Chasing Angels
And Failing Aristotle

By Michael Sinnes

Volume 1
Thesis Statement

To Brandi,
We'll always have Paris and "Knockin' on Heaven's Door."

Chasing Angels:
Never Sleep Alone

By Michael Sinnes

Prologue

He loved her like crazy, and she said, "You're my favorite." That was how it began, and that was how he always thought it would end. He always put her first, even with something as simple as referring to the two of them together in the third person. At night he told her: "'Sera and Holt' is lyrically better than 'Holt and Sera.' The latter is two trochaic feet. It begins on a high note and ends on a low one – much closer to the reality of life and love. On the other hand, 'Sera and Holt' is a trochee followed by an iamb – it begins on a high note and ends on one as well...that's us."

Each night was a new experience, a new high note. It never mattered that most nights contained this little lesson in lyric. She loved hearing it night in and night out as much as he loved saying it. It was his voice that got her in the beginning, and his stories. He caught her with a simple beginning – some high note of his past – a scene littered with detail so minute it was almost too much, but that was what made his stories so real. She was attentive through the long middle, riddled with events of the everyday and mundane – but still special because of the way he described them. He embellished tactfully and religiously. A 'couple' drinks were always 'too many,' and the mountain he described was a mile taller than the one he actually climbed. The decisions that drove the story forward were always the ones he should avoid, but they were the ones that best fit his personality – not the personality in the story, but, instead, the personality Sera saw when they were alone together. He never gave up on whatever ending he was shooting for, but, just when the story was about to reach its much deserved high note, Holt's stories ended in failure. Sera noticed.

Holt thought his life a tragedy rather than anything better. While he believed nothing could ever come between his wife and him, he always feared his own predilection to screw up. He lay awake with her at night telling her all these wonderful things about high notes and lyrical meter, but he wrote of failure in his stories. He was bound to fail at writing in the end. It was like he had the answers to all his questions for all these years, but he never listened to himself answer them. Sera knew this because he told stories in one of two ways: he either wrote exactly what he knew, or he wrote of his life as he wished it could be. When he wrote about what he knew he only wrote about past failures. When he wrote about some life he wished to live, he wrote only of the reasons why he could not have that life. Sera saw how hard he was on himself in his writing long ago, but she never said anything to him when he stopped writing altogether. He tried to make up for it. He became an agent, and a very successful one at that. They moved to New York and Holt moved right up the food chain at his agency – he was a shoe-in for partner. He was making shit loads as an agent, and he always believed he and Sera were happy together. Sure, he stopped writing, but he was making ten times what he could make as a writer. The fact he stopped writing was never a problem until he sold his truck.

His truck was in storage for years. Keeping the old pickup cost more than getting rid of it, and he sold it without talking to Sera. She knew how much he loved that truck. He lived in it for a while in college, and it was the only thing in the world he valued as highly as he valued Sera. She was pissed that he got rid of it. He didn't tell her about it because he needed money to surprise her with something – but he had two surprises. They had been fighting for days. He sold the truck on Monday and he had been bouncing back and forth between the bed and the couch ever since. It was Sunday already, but he had both his surprises with him as he went up the elevator. He told her he was working the weekend so he could take Monday off. Monday was their anniversary, and he had been working on his surprises non-stop. January sixteenth meant a lot to them. Not only had they met on that date, they also had their first wedding one year later on that same date. For the first time since they met he was going to give her an anniversary present on time. He needed to make up for this fight as soon as possible. He had no idea if they would survive another night. He planned on walking in and giving her his first surprise, information on an apartment at the Dakota – he just came from putting in an offer. She would finally understand the hiding things and sneaking around (She knew he would never cheat on her even if she had said it sounded like he was trying to pay a woman off in their last fight). Once the air was clear, he could show her his second surprise – the really good one. They would make up and, as they lay in bed, he would tell her it was another high note to get them through the low ones to come.

Tomorrow they would sleep in. He had trouble sleeping past the sunrise since he was a kid, but it was easy next to her. He always woke up right when the sun hit the window and he would watch Sera sleep for a minute or two. She had this layer of very thin blond hair covering her entire body. They were so small they were invisible unless his nose was against her skin, but they caught the early morning sun. It made her skin glow, just like an angel. He would take in the view for a minute and bury his face in her hair to shield his eyes from the sun. His face did not itch in her hair, and he always fell right back to sleep. It had been a week since he had a good night's sleep with his wife. He needed this fight to end.

He shook off his fear as he stepped off the elevator and walked down the hall to the corner apartment. The lights were off when he opened the door. He surveyed the space while he put his overcoat in the closet by the front door. The foyer light was enough to light the connected living room and dining area. When Sera came home from work she usually dropped her bag on the couch or the coffee table, but both were empty. She could have gone to her father's house in New Jersey. It was not unusual for Sera to stay there. It was a long commute from New York to her hometown where she taught high school. Her father lived minutes from the school, so sleeping there completely eliminated her commute. But she always called if she was staying there. When he looked at his phone, he didn't have any missed calls, voicemails, text messages, or emails.

Holt walked around the couch and loveseat, dropping his suit jacket and briefcase on the couch as he passed by. Once on the far side of the dining room he looked through the balcony's double doors to see if she was hiding outside. It was cold out and the balcony was empty. The kitchen was still dark. It looked like she never came home. Usually there would be dirty dishes in the sink when Holt came home late and a message that said 'I cooked dinner and leftovers are in the fridge' was scribbled on the magnetic, dry-erase board on the refrigerator door. There were no dishes. There was no sign of her at all. He walked back through the living room and down the hall toward the office and the bedroom. He noticed a sliver of light beneath the office door. The room was empty when he glanced inside. Everything looked fine in the bedroom as he continued through to the master bathroom. In there, Holt noticed something out of place. The master bathroom was Sera's bathroom. She always kept it very clean, and the only thing she ever left sitting out was the cup in which she kept her toothbrush. The cup always sat at the right corner of the sink, and it was missing.

While he did another lap through the house he gave Sera a call. The phone rang as he scanned the living room, the dining room, and the kitchen for a note or anything else out of the ordinary. After thirty seconds or so, her voicemail picked up. He left a message, "Give me a call, please," and hung up.

When he found nothing, he made his way back to the office. Although the toothbrush was missing, the photo of their first wedding was still sitting on her desk. He looked at the photo as he passed it. He was in a t-shirt and jeans – the dress code of his youth – and she was wearing his favorite shirt, a black thermal with a dark gray print. The collar was torn in the front, and the tear extended down into the design, just at the point where Sera's cleavage started. Holt always told her that he would tear it off her someday. He wanted to when they were arm in arm, standing in front of the Elvis impersonator who just married them in Vegas. Maybe it was a little cliché, but damn she looked good in that shirt. They went through with their formal wedding a few months later in New Jersey, but the one in Vegas – the one on January sixteenth – was the one they always counted. It would be ten years ago tomorrow. If that picture was still on that desk, there was hope that everything was okay. It was her prized possession, the only thing she valued as highly as she valued Holt.

The hope the picture instilled was short lived. He looked away from the picture, and saw a note on his desk. He was surprised to see it in the carriage of the typewriter he put away in their closet years before, but that was not the only surprise waiting for him on the desk. It was accompanied by a large manila envelope, adorned with ten stamps and two addresses written in Sera's handwriting. On top of the envelope was a silver ring – a ring as simple as the man that bought it. Holt stepped forward and sat in his desk chair. He leaned in toward the typewriter and fed the paper through so he could read the entire note.

"Apparently you left this envelope in the pickup when you sold it. You can imagine my surprise when the new owner dropped it off this evening. You forgot this ring on my finger, too. Just wanted to make sure you got them back."

Holt rested his elbows on the edge of the desk and cupped his face in his hands. His warm breath made his palms and face sticky as he tried to process the contents of the note. The envelope said it all. He knew what was inside. That was more than enough reason to leave. Holt forgot long ago the envelope even existed. There was no questioning it, his marriage was over.

After sitting like that for a few minutes, he kept his chin resting on his right palm as he examined the ring on his left hand. Holt gave Sera her silver ring back in college, but she started wearing it the day she first saw what was in the envelope. Sera gave him his silver ring the day the picture on her desk was taken. That same day she moved the silver ring from her right hand to her left. They put them on together and promised one another they would never take them off. It looked like they both lied about something.

Calling Sera again, Holt took the wedding picture off her desk and put it on his desk next to the envelope. The call went to voicemail after the second ring. He slipped the silver band off his finger, placing it on top of the envelope next to the other one. He stood from his desk, leaving the out-of-place items where they sat. Turning out the light and shutting the door, he left the office behind.

He walked to the kitchen and looked at the bottles of liquor in the cabinet by the refrigerator. His wife had some tequila, but he only drank Cuervo when Sera was around. He had some decent scotch, McCallan Fifteen, but that was only for entertaining guests. He reached up and grabbed the bottle of Jim Beam hidden behind the other bottles. He left the kitchen with the bottle of bourbon and a tumbler of water. In the living room he sat on the couch and opened his briefcase. The fliers for the Dakota fell to the floor as he pulled his second surprise out of the briefcase, a manuscript, <u>Failing Aristotle: the Unstoppable Force meets the Immovable Object</u>. He dropped the manuscript on the table as he cracked the seal on the bottle. He looked down the hall at the office door as he took two long gulps. The burn was inadequate punishment, so he let the whiskey lullaby go on before chasing the shot with a sip of water.

Failing Aristotle:

The Unstoppable Force
Meets the Immovable Object

By Holt Mallory

Lasciate ogne speranza, voi ch'intrate.

Dante's <u>Inferno</u>, Canto 3

Failing Aristotle

The Soundtrack 2 my Life

I had ninety-nine problems, and they were all Jessica. But, before you can understand the star-crossed nature of our relationship, I must first define for you the infinite difference between the unstoppable force and the immovable object. The universe is composed of two types of energy: kinetic and potential. Jessica can cross the universe in the width of a heartbeat. Her velocity makes her unstoppable – an object with unlimited kinetic energy. She gets what she wants and she destroys everything that gets in her way. She does so without malice, it's just her nature. I'm the only thing in the universe with the power to slow her down. I'm the immovable object, a single point of infinite potential. I can do anything – breach any limit. Like a black hole, I capture anything within my reach. Neither Jessica nor light can escape my gravity, but I destroy anything that gets too close. Jessica's was the only heart to survive my touch. When we collided, it was a two-way battle for survival. She realized she had the power to move me, and I found out how to catch her. I pray every day to this thing we call God that Jessica and I don't wind up on opposite sides of the same war. I fear the world would not survive. Maybe now you can understand our dilemma.

It was five months and some change since the last time I dropped her off in front of her Washington DC apartment. There was a time when you could have expected to see me parked out front in my Dakota every day – dropping Jess off, picking her up, or just coming to visit – but those times were long past. Up until two weeks ago, we hadn't spoken since New Year's Eve. I wasn't even sure she'd agree to meet when I texted her. Five months was a long time away from someone, especially someone with whom you've been so intimate. My greatest fear was that she'd have forgotten me altogether. I'd be lying if I said I didn't try to forget her every once in a while, but I didn't have the luxury of moving on like she did. We both knew I owed her something, something I promised her long ago. It was the only way I could ever let go of what happened, so maybe Jess and I could both move on.

I was surprised to see her sitting outside on the ledge by the west entrance when I pulled up. In the past, when I came to pick her up, I'd call her to let her know I was on the way, text her when I was half way to her apartment, call again before I turned into the driveway, and I'd still wind up waiting ten or fifteen minutes before she came out. It was a relief to know she wasn't going to leave me Waiting On A Woman once again. I waited for her too much since I met her. I tried to hide how much the waiting bothered me, but I couldn't help it sometimes. At least this Beautiful Mess was off to a good start.

She stood as the truck stopped. She was wearing that shirt I always liked, the black thermal with a tear down the front. It was a little warm for a black thermal in early May, but she was cold no matter what the situation. She hadn't worn that shirt in a long time. When she opened the door and crawled inside the back of the shirt separated from the top of her jeans. It gave the opportunity for a nice view of her lower back and the top of her butt crack. "Just get done workin' on the sink?" I asked.

She pulled the door shut and adjusted her pants when she was in the seat. After her bag was on the floor and she was buckled up, she backhanded me, pointing her finger as she said, "You deserved that."

"I was just pointing out the pants thing so you could fix it. I was doing you a favor."

"I didn't hit you for what you said. I hit you for looking in the first place."

"Jessica, did it ever cross your mind that hitting me is wrong?"

"No," she said as she turned her body and held out both her arms, inviting me in for a hug. I put the truck in park and looked behind us to make sure I wasn't blocking anyone in the circle drive before leaning toward her. Our hugs always started the same, a soft embrace, but they got tighter or softer depending on the silent message we wanted to send to one another. This time we just tried to Hold On Loosely. She buried her face where my shoulder and neck came together. My cheek rested against the side of her head, and I could see her hair blowing around in the breath from my nose. I turned and pressed my lips against the side of her head.

"I missed you, Mike," she said as she righted herself in the seat.

I put the truck in drive and pulled back onto Massachusetts Avenue, heading out of the District. I tried not to look at her as I said, "I missed you, too."

She turned half sideways in her seat and stared at me as I drove. There was something on her mind, but she always made me lead the conversations when things were awkward. "How've you been?" I asked.

"Good. Dad left town. He got out here a week ago. We played tourist for a few days and we had a really nice dinner last night after graduation." She trailed off on the last word as we passed The University. "I'm sorry you didn't graduate."

I took my eyes off the road and looked at the buildings on both sides of the street. They were supposed to look like stone buildings, but The University was too cheap to afford the real thing. They were just plaster over steel. "I'm not. I don't need a degree to write," I said as I put my eyes back on the road ahead.

"Are you gonna go back and finish?"

"No. I can't afford it, but it's nice to know you still worry about me."

"I never said I was worried about you. I think you're right. I'm just scared of how our story ends. All I know is that it can't bode well for me."

"I promised you a story-book ending a long time ago. I warned you that you might not like it."

"I guess I'll have to live with whatever I get." Her chin quivered with the last word.

"I'm sorry," I said, reaching across the truck and rubbing the back of her head with my finger tips.

"For what?"

"For shutting you out after the last time I saw you." I wiped away the solitary tear on her cheek, but I kept my eyes on the road as we crossed Western Avenue, the border between the District of Columbia and the state of Maryland. "I needed you out of my life to finish my book. It was the only way I could end this."

"I'm sorry, too. I'm sorry that I'm crying, and I'm sorry things went the way they did between us. I know this is my fault. I just hope the novel has a happy ending, that we get a happy ending." She opened up the glove compartment. "You still have my napkins in here," she said as she wiped her cheeks and blew her nose.

I turned off Massachusetts onto Westbard Avenue. My apartment was at the top of the hill. Jessica finished wiping her eyes and nose by the time I parked and she left the soiled napkins in the cup holder below the radio. I gave her a dirty look.

"I'll get 'em later," she said as she got out of the truck.

We walked across the parking lot side by side. I had my hands in my pockets as I walked and she kept her arms crossed, looking at the ground in front of her. "Can I ask you something?" she asked.

"You just did." I said, turning and looking at her with a half-smile. "You know you can ask me anything."

"You told me that you didn't want to be my friend while Matt and I were dating, but I told you Matt and I broke up on New Year's Eve. Why wouldn't you be my friend when he and I broke up?"

"I had to finish something."

"And I'm sure you nailed half the girls in DC in the process."

"I haven't touched a woman since the last time I spent the night with you." Considering the way that night ended, I wasn't sure if the look on her face was one of surprise or one of pity.

We walked up the stairs, and I opened the exterior door to the apartment, holding it open for her. I followed her through the door and we walked around the corner of the hall to my front door across from the elevator on the first floor. I pulled the key out of my pocket and slid it into the lock.

"Why did you want to see me today? Is the book finished?"

I paused before I turned the key. There were two ways to answer that question: I could flat out tell her the truth or I could open the door so she could see for herself. I looked at her a long time before I turned the key. "Please, don't hate me," I said as I pushed the door open.

She held my gaze as she walked through the door, but she froze when she looked inside. Her purse fell and she caught the shoulder strap in her hand. Her arms fell to her sides as she stared around the room. The opposite wall was nothing but windows – no love seat, television, or bar stools. The green granite counter tops in the kitchen were clean and bare. The couch that separated the foyer from the living room was gone. "Where the hell is all your stuff?" she asked.

I stepped through the door and stopped behind her, surveying the open space over her left shoulder. "I sold everything, I'm leaving town tomorrow."

"I thought your lease wasn't up until September. You can't leave. Where are you going? Why are you leaving? I don't want you to go." I tried to answer after every question, but I was interrupted with a new question. She kept rambling until she went quiet and threw her arms around me. She squeezed tight right from the start with her hands around my waist and her right ear pressed into my sternum.

I pulled my arms out of her hug so I could hug her back. I almost lifted her off the ground I squeezed so tight. "I gotta run away. Walls are caving in around me and it's time for me to go. I didn't want to leave without saying goodbye."

She spoke back, softly between broken tears, "You're my best friend. Please don't go. What about our second chance?"

"You're my best friend, too. That's why I wanted to spend my last night here with you – even if we don't spend the night together." We released and she stepped away to wipe away some fresh tears. It tore me up to see her cry, but it was a relief to know I was still worth a tear to her after everything we'd done to one another.

"I'm gonna miss you so much." She leaned forward and put a hand on each of my shoulders. After rising onto her toes, she gave me a soft kiss on the cheek. Just above the place her lips connected, I felt two tears: one from her cheek and one from my own eye.

I straightened up, maintaining my bearing. I couldn't let her see the second thoughts hiding Behind These Hazel Eyes. She lowered her purse to the floor as she stepped back from the kiss. "Can we smoke? I need to calm down after that bombshell."

I smiled and ushered her toward the kitchen. "I sold the computer and the computer desk. I have to roll it in here."

She sat on the counter as I opened the drawer to the right of the sink. I pulled out a little bag of weed, some papers, and a pair of scissors. I pulled a couple nuggets out of the baggie and started cutting them up.

Jessica watched as I worked on the joint. "Where are you going tomorrow?"

"Ft. Lauderdale to drop my truck off with a friend. After that I'm dropping off the radar."

"What happened to Colorado?"

"I finished something. Plans changed."

"I thought we were gonna run away to Colorado together?"

"That was before you broke up with me."

"What did you finish?"

"I don't have to tell you what you already know."

"I thought you were writing the book to get me back."

"I gave up on getting you back after your birthday."

When Jess saw I was finished with the joint, she slid off the counter. I walked toward the bedroom door, and she followed close behind. I held open the door and gave her a chance to look around the bare bedroom. The bed and both bookshelves were gone. I had my books packed in boxes and my two navy duffels full of clothes next to the empty closet. In the middle of the wall opposite the door, there was one pillow and my old fuzzy blanket off the couch. On the floor, by the wall of windows, there was a lone iPod dock and a cup I used as an ash tray. She stepped over by the iPod and took a seat. I sat on the opposite wall in the same corner. "Can I play some music?" she asked as she picked up the iPod.

"Mi casa es sous casa."

"This playlist has gotten longer since 'Summer 2009.' I appreciate the new music though."

"That was a good summer. It was…what…fourteen songs back then. I think it's like a hundred now." I lit the joint as she picked a song. I smiled as Buckcherry filled the air with the sound of "I'm Sorry."

"I figured this would be appropriate for both of us."

I passed her the joint. "Agreed," I said as I blew smoke out my nose and mouth.

After she took a hit, she lowered the joint and did a little jump where she sat. "I almost forgot what we were talking about. Where's my book? I know you're done with it already. I know you. You said you wouldn't speak to me again until it was finished. When you make a decision, you're immovable."

"If it were done, what makes you think I'd give it to you?"

"You want the story book ending just as much as I do."

She stared me down until I crawled across the floor to the boxes by the closet. I opened the top of the box on the far left and pulled out a large manila envelope. I resumed my seat in the corner by Jessica and sat the envelope on the floor to my right. We stared at each other as a Purple Haze filled the room. Montgomery Gentry came on the radio.

They begged for Speed but all I wanted was slow, nothing but slow. "Speed" always made me think of leaving girls behind, but I never thought I'd actually leave Jess behind.

I apologized for all the nights the worst of her memories got the Best Of Me when Jason Aldean came over the speakers. "You still drink like that?" she asked. "You scared the shit out of me when you started drinking again? I just pictured you winding up in the hospital again, or worse."

"I haven't had time to drink lately. I've been working full time and finishing this." I set my hand on the envelope.

"That novel." She pointed past me at the manila envelope on my right. "May I please see it? You're torturing me by dangling it in front of me. Are you enjoying this?"

"You could never begin to imagine how much I'm enjoying this." I picked myself up off the floor. I pulled a cigarette out of my pocket. "Can I trust you if I step out to smoke for a minute?"

She looked up at me through her eyebrows. Her eyes darted back and forth between my gaze and the envelope. "Do I have to be good?"

"If you're going to look at the novel, go to the last page first, please. I'm not just giving you permission. It's an order."

"Aye-aye, captain." She held her right hand to her brow in a shamefully poor salute. "You gotta have your story book ending don't you?"

"You want this ending, too. Just be the bull and let it happen," I said as I pulled the door shut behind me. In the bathroom I leaned in close to the mirror, looking into my own eyes. I knew the feeling in the pit of my stomach was fear. I'd felt it before. In moments like this, when I got scared, I never really understood what was going through my head. I'd felt fear before, but years of compartmentalizing emotion gave me the ability to ignore it altogether – I was practically a sociopath, but in the good way. The only way to have power over fear was by not letting it have any power over me. Still, I was compelled to try and look inside my eyes to understand my fear. I was a soul gazer. I could see inside someone's mind through their eyes. I've never really understood how it works, but it never worked when I tried to do it to myself. The only things visible were the two colors of my irises: the brown ring around

15

my pupil and the hazel that surrounded it. It looked to me like I had no soul – like I wasn't human.

I was about to get the only thing I ever wanted, but there was no way Jessica was getting into that truck with me the next day. I had to do the next part alone. I had to leave her behind to conquer the world. I couldn't be scared anymore. I'd spent all this time writing a book trying to figure out how someone actually goes about conquering the world, but Jessica taught me the book was the answer I sought. I'd been writing the book to get her back, but the book became my weapon for global conquest. I'd been trying to conquer the world to prove to myself that I actually deserved her – that I deserved my gifts. I liked to call them my superpowers.

Jessica, however, was my Kryptonite since the moment I met her. Whenever I looked into her eyes I just got lost. No one else could bullshit me, even a little, but she successfully lied to me multiple times. Leaving her behind to conquer the world was the only logical choice. I had to be at my best when it came to playing this most dangerous of games.

When I walked back into the bedroom, she was sitting in the same spot with the novel in her hand. It was open to the last page, and she'd drifted into her thousand yard stare. She closed the novel and reached for the iPod. She ran out of the room as our song started, but she was only gone a few seconds before she came back with her purse. I knew what kind of mess was in there. If she was looking for anything smaller than a pack of cigarettes she might as well give up. Somehow she proved me wrong, pulling out a silver ring – a ring as simple as me – and slipping it on her right hand.

I held out my hand, offering to take her back to that place in my heart where nobody's been. She grabbed my hand and offered to Take Me There, too. I pulled her close and wrapped my arms softly around her waist. She lifted her hands and rested her arms on my shoulders. Her right hand gripped the hair on the back of my head and she leaned her head into my chest. We hadn't danced to our song since the first time we heard it, ten feet from Rascal Flatts.

"That's not my book."

"I had to finish <u>Chasing Angels</u>. The last time you were here, I realized I couldn't finish the novel until I understood where the novel came from, the part of me that inspired it. What I just gave you is what came after. <u>Chasing Angels</u> is still in there, but now it has its other half. Together they're my resume to conquer the world."

"Still planning to take over the world?"

"Of course. This book is how I'm gonna do it."

"Always the idealist. I get to keep this copy, right."

"It's yours."

"Are you gonna publish it with that note to me at the end."

"I was planning on it."

"Did you mean it?"

"I meant it every time I said it before and I still do. That will never change."

"Everything's changed."

"I know."

"My answer's yes…to your note. Yes."

"I knew that when I saw the ring."

We tried to keep dancing, but we weren't really moving to begin with. We just swayed slowly back and forth until the song ended. As the music faded away, we drifted apart, but we kept our hands on one another – her hands on my shoulders and mine around her waist. We saw the last two years between us, but that all faded away in an instant. Relativity shifted as the space and time between us was reduced to zero. We hit light speed. Modern Mathematics break down at the speed of light, but we were just getting started. Neutrinos would have been amazed at the speed with which we moved through one another. Time contracted around us as we dilated. She became my whole world and for a while I was all hers. Logic couldn't explain what happened between us. The world didn't move because we dwarfed the world as we moved. Time couldn't stop because we ignored its passage altogether. We danced outside definable space where God, love, and infinity exist. The only words to describe what happened between us were everything and nothing.

When nothing was over we wrapped ourselves in the fuzzy blanket on the floor. Our clothes were scattered and her shirt was draped over my duffel bags, torn right down the front. We kept our bodies pressed together and did our best to share the pillow. "I'm sorry we're sleeping on a floor again. You Deserve Much Better Than Me."

"Michael, do you remember Nevada? I told you a long time ago I don't care where I sleep with you. As long as I'm with you I'll sleep well."

We did.

I had to leave early the next morning. I left Jessica asleep on the floor as I packed the boxes and bags into my truck. The sun would be up in an hour and I wanted to be on my way out of the city before rush hour set in. All I had left to do after loading the truck was taking Jess home. When I woke her up, she got dressed in silence. She was never much of a morning person, but today was different. She didn't yell at me once.

I gave her my old blue Navy hoodie to take the place of her shirt. She put it on without saying a word. We went out to the truck and she sat quietly in the seat as we drove out of the parking lot and down the hill toward Massachusetts Avenue. There were a couple cars on the road as we headed south toward the District through the suburbs of Maryland. We passed through Westmoreland circle, crossing the state line back into the District. She kept her eyes fixed out the passenger window. I wanted to say something, but the only thing I could think to say was 'I Got Nothin'.' I figured saying nothing was better than saying the wrong thing. And the wrong thing was my specialty in situations like that one.

"Can you pull around back and park?" she asked as I turned toward her apartment. "I just don't want to say goodbye yet."

"This isn't goodbye." Instead of going left into the apartment's circle drive, I turned right and pulled around the back of the building. I found a spot by the rear entrance and parked. We got out and took a seat on the tailgate. I pulled out two cigarettes and lit them both.

She pulled on the cigarette and rubbed on the side of the truck bed. "I'm gonna miss you, Dakota."

"She's a good truck."

"The best."

"You know, I'm gonna name my first kid after my truck."

"We'll see about that. Dakota is a great name – and its gender neutral – but that's pretty redneck. Think of the kid."

"I can't deny who I am."

"I wouldn't want you to." She looked at me for a long time. I looked back, but I didn't say anything. I wanted to make sure she had every chance to say what she wanted to say. "I'm gonna miss you, too, Mike. I really am. I decided to stay in DC this summer because I wanted to be your friend, at a minimum. Hell, I even thought we might give this" she pointed back and forth between us "another chance. I thought we might try and conquer the world together, but I understand why you're leaving."

"We will conquer the world together. It's your resume, too." I pointed at the envelope sticking out the top of her purse. I flicked my cigarette into the parking lot and stood to face her. She dropped her cigarette butt as she stood and stepped it out. I put my arms around her and gave her a kiss. We held each other for a long time after. "This isn't goodbye," I said again.

"Then what the hell is it?" she asked through broken tears.

"See You When I See You." We let go of one another, and took a step back to get a good last look, trying to find comfort in the thought that it was far from over between us. "And I hope to see you real soon."

"I'm coming after you." Her chin quivered as she spoke.

"You promise?" I cried, too.

She backed away from me and held her right hand in the air. Her fingers were balled into a fist, but she kept her pinky pointing straight. I locked my pinky in hers and we both kissed our thumbs. We used the interlocked fingers to pull ourselves together and finish the pinky-promise with one long, last kiss. When we were done, she backed up onto the sidewalk and I got back in the truck. I stared at her as I backed out of the parking spot. She didn't move, so I stopped and rolled down the window. I leaned out and yelled, "Jess, I love you like crazy."

"You're my favorite."

That was all the story book ending I'd ever need. I gave her a half nod as I drove away. Rounding the back of the apartment I rubbed the dashboard of my truck, whispering to the steering wheel, "Bring me that horizon." I kept from looking in the mirrors for as long as possible. I knew what I'd see if I looked back, but it wasn't the distance I feared. What I feared was More Than Miles. I had to run from the sun setting on Jess and me. I sped south down Foxhall Road to get to the Key Bridge in Georgetown. From there it was a straight shot south on I-95 to Florida. I'd have all the speed in the world to leave Jess behind on the highway. As I merged onto the interstate, I caught a mean glare from my rear-view. It was like the light of an angel behind me screaming out What I Need To Do. But I didn't see Jessica when I looked to identify the light. The only thing I saw was the sun rising, as it also does.

Chapter 1

Holt's face never itched in his dreams. He remembered that as he rubbed his face, but rubbing only made the itch worse. As he opened his eyes he felt hair stuck in his whiskers. He looked for his right hand but it was trapped beneath a sea of long red hair washing away from the soft taper of a woman's shoulders and down her back with curls as wild as the shore during high tide in a hurricane. Without his right hand he had to roll onto his back and brush the hair over Alex's shoulder to free his face from the itchy locks. By the time the hair was clear, he was awake enough to realize he just woke up. He stared at the ceiling and took a couple deep breaths to get his bearings. It took a minute for his brain to boot up and he looked back at Alex.

When they slept together before, one person or the other woke for work before the sun came up, but today was different. They grabbed drinks the night before and did once more what they both promised to never do again. Both slept straight through the sunrise. As the light shone through the bedroom's wide picture window the light refracted off her alabaster skin like a prism. The soft light filled the room, but cast no shadows. This was the first time Holt saw her angelic glow in the early morning sun.

He fell in love with her hair before they were physical, and he examined the freckles across her body countless times since they started sleeping together. A group on her back formed Orion if the constellation faced east instead of west in the sky. There was another line of freckles running up one arm across the back of her shoulders and down the other arm. These freckles were smaller and they made a nice background for the constellation. Her back looked like the night sky if the backdrop of night was as bright as the sun and the stars were dark against it.

His left hand followed the freckles up her arm and over her shoulder. Leaning in close he whispered, "I gotta get my arm."

She tossed her hair back over her shoulder and into his face as he spoke. He kissed her neck where it met her shoulder through a mouthful of hair. He did a hug and roll to get his sleepy right arm out from under her neck. He laid her back on the bed, and a single, narrowed, green eye glared over her shoulder. "I threw my hair back because my face

21

itched," she said as she got comfortable again. "I didn't mean to hit you."

"Yes you did." He slid toward the edge of the bed and sat up.

"Maybe I meant it a little. I'm sorry, coffee."

He knew what it meant when Alex addressed him as coffee, so he looked around for his clothes. Undressing was his favorite activity in the bedroom. His typical modus operandi was to pull an article of clothing off a woman and toss it without thinking. His tendency to undress a woman wildly often incited this wild tendency in the woman as well. There were mornings when his bedroom was a mess of blankets, pillows, and clothes strewn about without remorse. Sometimes clothes were lost altogether. His shirt landed on the vanity by the window, and his boxers were next to the bed. His pants, however, were not so easy to find. His memory was a little hazy from the previous night's celebration, so he stood from the bed and checked the bathroom. The bathroom was not as pristine since Holt took over the space, but he could tell in a single sweep with his eyes that his pants were elsewhere. He walked through the bedroom door and into the hallway. He stepped quickly as he travelled down the hall, his feet cold against the hardwood floor. His pants were halfway down the hall just outside the office. He pulled them on and felt inside the pockets for his cigarettes and lighter. He started the coffee pot as he passed through the kitchen on his way to the balcony.

Outside the UN looked small across the East River, and he could almost see straight down 47th street into Times Square. Holt's gaze travelled from the Brooklyn Bridge to the north side of Manhattan. The skyscrapers looked like blades of uncut grass against the sky, but no natural green was visible. The view he had from his apartment in Queens almost did justice to the size of New York. A year ago he thought he would never leave this city. No one could explore the city in a lifetime, but he planned on spending the rest of his life trying to with his wife – before she left. Central Park was hidden behind the mess of buildings, but he knew the general direction. The condo would be sold in another week and that was where he was planning to move for some time.

When he got back to the bedroom, Alex was already out of bed. He heard the water running through the open bathroom door. Her silhouette shone through the smoked glass of the shower door. She had a dancer's figure: long, lean, and muscular. It was a perfect hourglass from her shoulders down to the narrow waist where her body exploded into a great ass. When she sat, her upper body rested on thirty-eight inches of solid muscle, and she had legs to match.

"I put on coffee like you asked."

"Sorry. I looked at my phone and I have to start getting ready for work. Get in here."

"I'll get in the shower if you stay and have breakfast." He undid his pants, but he waited without dropping them.

"I'm already late and I have a lot of work to finish today. You need to get ready for work, too."

"Last time I checked I'm still your boss. You can be late. I'll tell them a client had an emergency."

"People know we went out for drinks last night. They might think something's going on between us."

"Something is going on."

"We don't want them to find out."

"People at the office are far too self-absorbed to notice that anything is going on in other people's lives. We've got the perfect excuse and we've never had breakfast together."

Her arms fell to her side. "You're cooking…and cleaning."

"Deal." Holt let go of his pants as he raced to the shower door. He stepped straight under the stream of hot water as Alex shampooed her hair. The shower had reduced the raging torrent of her curls to the soft waves of a calm sea. She turned away from him and shrugged her shoulders a couple times as she soaped the long tail of hair over her shoulder. He blocked the stream of water with his back as he rubbed her shoulders, running his firm grip down her back. Her hands scrubbed her scalp slower and slower the harder he rubbed her body.

"Let me rinse my hair out," she said over her shoulder. They switched places. She put her back under the stream and leaned her head back into the water. He rubbed the water and suds down the front half of her body. He started at her shoulders and he had to bend over when he rinsed her stomach, hips and legs.

When she was done rinsing her hair, she stepped to the side and pushed Holt under the stream of water. He put his hands against the wall and leaned forward. The water ran down his back, and she rubbed him down from shoulders to calves. "What's with this tattoo on your back – the cross?"

"It's a secret."

"I only ask because Mike didn't have that tattoo in your book. He had Dickens. He had Donne. He had Virgil and Caesar. He even had 'True to thyself' tattooed in the same place on his chest. He had all the same tattoos as you except that cross on your back. What's so special about that one?"

"It was the last tattoo I got. I got all the lettering done when I was in college. I got the cross a year later, when I ran away to Colorado."

"What's the secret?"

"Something I was supposed to do."

"Elaborate."

"I was supposed to mail something."

"Does Sera know?"

"You don't feel weird talking about my ex-wife?"

"Well, you're not divorced yet, and we were friends while you were married. How long have we worked together?"

"Seven years, five months, and six days…give or take."

She paused at the accuracy of the response. "How long ago did we first sleep together?"

"Four months and a couple days, when I showed you my manuscript. I can't seem to find that, by the way."

"I don't know what to tell you about the manuscript. And stop changing the subject. As far as I'm concerned we're friends first, co-workers second, and sex comes in a close third. I can handle talking about Sera. I know how much she meant to you, and I've tried to be there for you the best I can."

"I thought last night was supposed to be the last time…again?"

"But you're still a dear friend. Did you ever tell Sera about the cross?"

"She knew, and she left the day she found what I didn't mail."

"What was it?"

"It doesn't matter."

"It must've been something serious. Have you two spoken since she left? You've never really talked about it."

"She tried calling once but…I missed the call."

"You were fucking Brandi." She leaned over his shoulder as he looked back. Their eyes met and she raised her eyebrows at him. "Don't worry. I know we're not exclusive."

"It was weird, though. The message she left sounded like she was coming home. I tried calling back the next day. She picked up and told me she never wanted to speak again – that she wanted a divorce. That was all I got."

"You gotta buck up." She stood him up straight as she poured body wash on his shoulders. Her hand was there to spread the cold soap around as soon as it hit his back. She rubbed the soap around in long, firm strokes. She followed the ridge of his spine, rubbing the muscles on either side. She rubbed his shoulders starting at his neck and moving outward. When she got to his arms, he flexed his triceps and she grabbed hold of the tightened muscles. He looked back over his shoulder and she returned the gaze with hungry eyes. She washed down his lower back and hurried below his waist. She turned him around and repeated the process on his front. She took her time on that half.

When she finished him off, Holt turned under the water to rinse off and traded places with Alex again. He rinsed her front and back, spinning her as he did so. He pulled her out from under the water and put three blobs of soap on her chest. He washed her from top to bottom and made sure to hit all the important parts, but he hurried through washing her front half. They were short on time. He turned her around and put soap on her shoulders. He had to put in time on her back.

"If there's one thing I'm gonna miss about fucking you, it's your hands."

"What about 'em?" He spread the soap across her back. His hands crossed her shoulders from scapula to clavicle. He squeezed one side and then the other with a steady rhythm.

"That," she moaned. "Your hands are soft to the touch, but they're so damn strong. You have a real man's hands, tough yet gentle. Your hands are definitely your best feature." She put both her hands against the shower wall as he rubbed down the length of her back. His hands moved with his thumbs pointing toward the ridge of her spine and the fingers on both his hands pointing toward the outside of her back. His hands slid down quickly and gently, but they pushed up slowly and firmly, following the direction of the trapezius muscle – up and out – as they moved.

"I'm gonna miss your backrubs."

"It's not like we'll never see each other again. Unless you're gonna stop being my assistant." He rubbed her lower back, squeezing the point where her waist transitioned out and rubbed his thumbs in the dimples at the small of her back.

"I don't think it's appropriate for me to keep sleeping with my boss."

"You've got a point, but the sex is good." He soaped her down to her ankles. He took his time washing the length of each leg, making sure to give the long muscles a relieving rub.

"That's an understatement." She stepped under the water as Holt stood back up. "I knew we were a bad idea the first time we slept together. I was rebounding from my ex and Sera had just left you. It is what it is – or was what it was – whatever. I think we'll be fine going back to our normal, friendly, working relationship." She stepped out of the shower and grabbed a towel off the rack. Holt shut off the water and followed her out.

They walked out of the bathroom to finish drying off. He went to the closet and slid open the right door. He tried to ignore the other, empty half of the closet as he rummaged through his half. He pulled a lavender button-up and a pair of khakis off their hangers and got a pair of boxers out of the dresser. He was planning on wearing them with a blue blazer, but he didn't need a tie. He could just call it casual Friday. He buttoned the shirt and watched Alex dress as he put on socks and shoes. She had on a pair of white boy-shorts with orange trim and orange polka dots. She donned her matching bra backwards around her waist. Once it was fastened, she spun it around and threw the straps over her shoulder, adjusting her chest as she went. She looked around the room spinning as she did so and caught Holt staring at her.

"Enjoying the show?"

"Very much so."

"Where is my dress?"

Holt gave the room a quick once over. It wasn't on the floor and it did not look like the dress landed on any of the bedroom furniture. He walked to the foot of the bed and grabbed the comforter by the corners.

26

He snapped it in the air like he was spreading a tablecloth. The comforter paused before falling, supported by the air beneath. Alex dove beneath the gentle fall of the blanket when she saw her dress fall to the mattress.

"Neat trick," she said as she crawled out from under the blanket.

"I've lost a few dresses in my day." He sounded pleased with himself as he spoke. She rolled her eyes and turned away, throwing the dress over her head and letting it fall around her body. Alex grabbed her shoes off the floor and followed Holt out of the bedroom and down the hallway.

He walked to the kitchen and turned on the stove. Alex poured them both a cup of coffee and sat on the counter next to the stove as Holt got a skillet and a couple plates out of the cabinet. He grabbed eggs, sausage, and butter out of the refrigerator and put them on the counter next to the stove opposite Alex. He put some butter in the skillet and unpacked the sausages as the butter melted, rolling his sleeves halfway up his forearm to keep the grease from staining his shirt cuffs.

Alex looked at the bottom half of Holt's tattoos, visible now that his sleeves were rolled up. "If I'm staying for breakfast, you're answering one question."

"We agreed that you would stay for breakfast if I took a shower with you."

"We're renegotiating. I still have something you want and there's something else I want now. Deal with it."

"You'll make one hell of an agent someday."

"Why do you keep your tattoos covered? I didn't even know you had tattoos until–"

"You took my clothes off."

"Exactly. This is the only time I've ever seen your tattoos when you have clothes on. Why keep them covered?"

"In our profession people aren't always receptive to tattoos."

"You're not an agent when you're not at work. You can show off those tattoos as much as you want when you're not in the office, but you don't. You still wear long sleeve button-ups with the sleeves rolled down. Those tattoos are a part of you few people see – the best part of you. The sleeve on your left arm is like your shield, and the two lines of Latin on your right arm are your sword. They're actually pretty fuckin' bad ass." She reached down to the plate of sausages Holt just finished. He was using both hands to flip the eggs, so he had no way to prevent her from stealing a bite.

"Can you start some toast?" She slid off the counter to do what he asked as he continued. "I've just kept them hidden for so long as an agent I've gotten used to keeping them covered. When I got them I was supposed to be a rebel – that's what most people called me. I was strictly a jeans and t-shirt guy back then, but that was a long time ago. I'm a business man now."

"Wrong. You may have everyone else fooled, but I know you're just pretending to be an agent. If I remember right we slept together right after I read your novel for the first time. You're a writer. Isn't that what you told me you wanted to be back in your rebellious days? Do you even own a t-shirt and jeans anymore?"

Holt slid the eggs out of the skillet onto two plates. He split the sausages into two stacks. He made sure that he put the one out of which she took a bite onto his plate. She would be less likely to steal his food if he gave her more than he gave himself. "A sword and shield? I don't think anyone has ever referred to my tattoos like that before."

"You're avoiding the question, avoider. No one talks about them because no one ever sees them." When he set the skillet down, she grabbed him by both arms and turned him to face her. "I love these two in Latin. They're so…Holt. God the first time we had sex, I saw your tattoos and I swear my clothes just melted off me. I know we aren't together, but I want you to do me a favor, as a friend: don't keep these covered all the time." She ran her hands over the ink on both his arms. "You started hiding from who you were a long time ago. In the end, that's why Sera left – not because of some stupid secret. That was the straw that broke the camel's back, but that wasn't the reason. I know I'm overstepping my bounds as some girl you're fucking, but you're a great guy. The only reason I can see your wife leaving is because you're so scared of the things about you that don't fit the status quo. I was the first person to read your book and I know you're so far from the status quo that you're a class all your own. That novel is who you are, or were, and writing it was a step in the right direction. You need to be yourself again. I'm sorry, but you needed to hear it."

Holt picked up the plates and motioned toward the dining room table. "You're not overstepping any boundaries. You're one of the few people I know I can call that'll always pick up. I don't have many friends in my life anymore, so you can say whatever you need or want to say. That's why I wanted you to read my book – but you weren't the first to read it."

"Who was the first? Oh yeah…Brandi." She rolled her eyes as she said the name.

"Sera, too." Holt kicked up one eyebrow and took a bite.

"When did she read it? You told me you had just finished writing it when she left."

"It was a long time ago. I wrote the novel back in college. I don't have the original manuscript anymore. I re-wrote the whole thing from memory right before she left. What you read was the re-write."

"Obviously I loved it." She looked down at her clothes. "You think anyone will notice if I go into work wearing the same clothes from yesterday?"

"You're pretty easy on the eyes. I'm not trying to take away from your qualifications, but I know I'm not the only guy in the office that checks you out. Someone would definitely notice."

"Are you saying you hired me because you wanted to sleep with me?"

"I hired you because you were qualified, but your looks didn't hurt your chances at getting the job. When we were both copy-editors all the agents were jealous that we spent all our time in the break room together. We were both due for a promotion and I didn't want one of the assholes that would actually try and sleep with you taking you on as their assistant."

"And look what happened: we started sleeping together."

"In my defense I never thought about sleeping with you until the night you showed up at my door and started making out with me."

"What can I say? I love your writing."

"My four favorite words in the English language."

"I've gotta call the office." Alex scraped the last of her food onto Holt's plate as she stepped away from the table and walked out onto the balcony. Holt finished eating as she talked to their boss. "No, I was gonna bring my surprise for Holt but I forgot it at home. I've got to run

29

back and pick it up. I should be in the office in about an hour or so. I called Holt to let him know and he said he's gonna be late, too." She listened to the phone for a few minutes as she paced the length of the balcony. "I don't know when he's gonna be in. He said he had to stop by the bank before he meets with his realtor this afternoon." As she said the word 'realtor' she opened her mouth, stuck her tongue out, and pointed down the back of her throat with her index finger.

She finished her call and moved back toward the table. She reached for her plate, but Holt grabbed it. "I told you I would clean up." He left her coffee cup on the table and started toward the kitchen with all the dirty dishes. It only took a minute to finish washing everything and load the dish washer. He poured the rest of his coffee into the sink and broke down the coffee pot. Alex walked to Holt and handed him her empty coffee cup.

"What do you have for me at your place?" he asked as he put the last dish on the rack and started the machine.

"You'll have to wait and see when you get to work." She turned and began walking slowly toward the door, extending her arm and swinging her purse by the shoulder strap.

Holt followed her toward the door. "Just tell me. I hate surprises."

"No one hates surprises." As she spoke, she pulled open the front door. They were both startled by a man standing on the other side. His right hand was raised as if he were about to knock. He was wearing a black suit and a black tie with a white shirt underneath. He could have passed for a government agent or a mortician, not much else.

The man lowered his right hand into his inside jacket pocket. "Holt Mallory?"

Holt stepped in front of Alex. "Yeah, can I help you?"

"Just did." He pulled a blue, tri-folded piece of paper out of his pocket and handed it to Holt. "You've been served."

Holt unfolded the blue affidavit. He read the first lines of the white, front page: "Motion for the dissolution of marriage in the state of New Jersey. Sera Mallory v. Holt Mallory."

"Miss Mallory asked that I give you this as well." The man pulled a brown box from behind his back. He somehow hid it from view with his left hand. Once the package was in Holt's hand, the stranger disappeared down the hall.

Holt let the door fall shut as he looked over the box and the divorce papers. "That was surprising."

"Is that what I think it is?" Alex asked.

Holt refolded the divorce papers and returned Alex's gaze, giving her a quick nod.

Alex stepped close and wrapped her arms around him, squeezing him tight as she lifted herself onto her toes. "I'm sorry, Holt. Do you want me to stay a little longer? We could take the day off."

"No, I'm fine. I knew these would come eventually. I'll see you at the office in a bit. I think I'm gonna need your surprise to cheer me up."

"Can't wait. See you soon." They gave each other a quick hug and a kiss on the cheek. She looked over her shoulder before walking out the door. "It'll be okay, Holt. I promise."

Holt took a seat on the couch, dropping the divorce papers on the coffee table. He set the brown box in his lap. It was light and unwrapped. Its top face was about the size and shape of construction paper, and the box was only a couple inches thick. Each side of the lid was attached to the bottom of the box with a single piece of tape. Holt cut the tape with his keys. When he lifted the lid off the box, two words were staring him back in the face: 'Billa' and 'Bong.' It was his old backpack from college. 'Billa' was embroidered on the right shoulder strap and 'Bong' was embroidered on the left. It was designed so the brand name, Billabong, was visible when the wearer had both straps on. He lifted the bag out of the box. Both compartments were unzipped and the frayed interior fabric was loose in the box. It was old, but it was still a good bag – no matter how much Sera tried to make him get rid of it. There was nothing inside the backpack, but there was a note in the bottom of the box: "I borrowed this a few months ago. I know how special this is to you."

Holt wadded up the note and dropped it back in the box. He set the bag on the couch as he carried the box toward the kitchen. When the box and note were in the trash he walked onto the balcony. He lit a cigarette and stared out over the East River. He only smoked half the cigarette before he said, "Fuck you, Sera," flicking his cigarette over the edge of the balcony toward the water.

Graduate

"Can I Graduate?" I asked the bastards, but I knew the three of them would never listen. Any man in his right mind would have given up and bowed out of this fight, but I've never been a man in his right mind. I wasn't scared to face an uphill battle. It may not have been the correct course of action, but at least I had a sense of honor about me.

These days, few people are familiar with honor. The presence of honor is not dependent upon morality, but the learning curve of all honorable people involves balancing courage with prudence. Courage drives honorable men to fight unwinnable battles, but prudence guides them to peace in the face of a winnable one. I overlooked prudence facing this unwinnable battle for the sake of the honorable man sitting next to the bastards, Professor Styles. He worked for The University the same as the other three, but he was the one that set up this meeting. He'd come into my bar around Closing Time a couple weeks earlier and found out that I'd dropped out of school. When he accused me of giving up I told him about the book I'd written and that I'd accept a degree from The University if they'd accept the work I'd done as my last semester of college. I figured he dropped it the second he walked out of my bar, but the millionaire K Street attorney in him must've taken over. He called me a week later and told me he'd set up a meeting. He even squeezed it in before finals so maybe I could graduate on time. I knew it was a hopeless fight from the get-go, but I showed up anyway. Although I was aware he was an honorable man, I had to make sure he knew I was, too – as men of honor often do.

The room was filled by a large, four-piece, circular table. I sat on one side, and The University staff sat diametrically opposite me. I knew two of the three bastards sitting next to Professor Styles. I'd taken Professor Dikface's senior level creative writing workshop a year earlier. Professor Dooshback was the head of the Literature Department. She was a literary academic. I'd taken her class the previous fall in which I was supposed to write my undergraduate thesis. Those two didn't think very highly of me, but, based on past encounters, I'd lost all respect for them.

Speaking of no respect, let's move on to the last of the bastards. He never even had the common decency to introduce himself, so I'll just call him the Administrator. He was middle aged and he looked pretty generic in khakis, a white button up, and a blue blazer with the gold buttons on the cuffs. I'd run into his type on a few occasions, but I was careful to avoid them whenever I could. Case in point, the last time I talked to an administrator I dropped out of school. My main reason for disliking the administrative type was their incapacity for looking me in the eye. They always looked at their notes, a computer screen, or the floor when they talked to me. Giving them the benefit of the doubt, I justified their inability to look me in the eye by telling myself they were intimidated by me, but administrators truly cared more about what's on paper than the reality around them. I've met exceptions to this rule. One example was the previous Dean of Students. She was a genuinely good person – a rarity at The University. She left my junior year. I never heard why she left. I just figured it was the same reason that every other worthwhile person left – there was no room for good people. When I heard she'd left, I knew it was only a matter of time before I followed suit. She was my last line of defense against an education system unfamiliar with non-traditional students like me. Without her I was left with administrators like the chode on my right.

I'd already been in the meeting for twenty minutes surveying the field of battle. Dooshback and Dikface had a tendency of getting on my nerves, but I could see more on a White Blank Page than I could find in their heads. I became familiar with their narrow minds and one-dimensional personalities when I took their respective classes. They said little of substance then, and they hadn't changed since. They both spoke to hear themselves speak, but I entertained their dialogue out of respect for Professor Styles. There was no way I'd allow their shortcomings to dictate my future.

"Can I graduate?" I asked again. The bastards had been looking back and forth at one another since the first time I asked. If you've ever seen the look on a baby's face when they first learn to consciously take a dump, then you'd know what I was dealing with. "I'm not asking to walk at the graduation ceremony. I'm not asking to get a diploma or a degree. All I need is nine more credits added to my transcript. That way I don't have to pay back the Department of Veteran's Affairs all the money they paid for the education I didn't receive."

Failing Aristotle

Dikface leaned forward in his chair. "Michael, I really want to see you graduate," lying, two-faced, cock stain, "but, before I can make a decision whether this manuscript is worthy of credit, we need to discuss something." I knew exactly what he was about to say. He asked this same question about everything he read: "What does it mean?"

I closed my eyes and took a deep breath, pinching the bridge of my nose to ward off the migraine his stupidity brought on. "Meaning is outside the scope of the author. It's derived in the mind of the reader – it's a singular concept. Writing is an exploration in plurality. What means one thing to the writer could mean something different to each individual reader. The novel means something to me, but that doesn't matter. I wrote the novel about five girls I dated after I left Kansas. I want to make sure they all know how much they meant to me – what they still mean to me. The metaphors and meaning are little more than fodder for academics. It can mean whatever you want it to, because I have no intention of reading it ever again. I wrote it, so I've read it enough already."

"I'm the head of the Creative Writing Department and I wrote two novels. I was able to put meaning on the page," he fluttered his eyes and sat up extra straight as he spoke the last sentence. Having spent some time between the covers of his novels, the fact he was a virgin made a lot more sense to me. They were hard to find, and, in summation, the one I skimmed was the retarded love child of Jason Bourne and Harry Potter – with a little bit of vampire crap added in.

"Congrats." I got comfortable in my chair, deciding to have a little fun. "I thumbed through one of your books a few months back. Really hard to find, you know, but, once I actually found it, I gave it a look."

Styles leaned forward in his chair. He raised his thick eyebrows and pointed a finger at me as he said, "Watch it, Mike."

I mouthed the word 'sorry' as I sat back up in my chair. I resumed my good, seated posture. "As a writer, I try to lay down meaning that I think people will find. I want people to see the world through my eyes. Hopefully my audience will come to recognize the same flaws I've found in the world around me. For example: throughout the novel, I compare divorce and selling an apartment. Both are legal issues with similar paperwork, but divorce is easier than selling a house because of the world's financial state. I can get married and divorced ten times in

34

the time it may take me to sell a house. This is the world that my generation is left with, and I'll be honest, my generation is fucked. To start with, your generation" I pointed to the four people across from me "failed at raising mine. I like to call my generation the 'worthless generation' because you're the only example we've had to follow. There are exceptions to this rule – I've met many people my age of great worth – but the vast majority of my generation isn't ready for the real world. You coddled us too much. You taught us to tattle-tale on a bully rather than fight back. You told us we can be anything we want to be, but you failed to mention that some people are just meant to be garbage men. I didn't write a novel. I wrote a resume to lead my generation, because they need someone to look up to. They need someone to be honest with them about the world. They need to be shown how to fight back when the world knocks them down. They need someone that can think for himself and teach them how to think for themselves. These are the 'meanings'" I made finger quotes in the air "that I wanted to come through in the writing."

"That gives me a clear idea of your intention with the writing, but where does the meaning fit into genre?"

I was well aware of the fact that Dikface was pretty dumb. When I took his class, I wrote a riddle to see if he was smart enough to get the answer if the answer was written at the top of the page. When he was the only person that didn't figure it out, I laughed out loud and everyone else joined in. You've got to love life's little victories, but he won that round in the end.

"I don't like to apply genre to text," I started. "Genre limits a text by narrowing its scope. If I were going to say anything, this novel is romantic in nature – a text of the everyday and mundane to put it into a Wordsworthian school of thought. When I sat down to write this I was very concerned with the ideas of similitude and dissimilitude, because people tend to identify with a text in one of two ways: they associate themselves with the character traits they find similar to themselves, and they dissociate themselves from the traits they find dissimilar. I wrote this novel with the idea of getting inside the mind of my audience, because that's what writing is all about. I had to look inside myself and find the parts of myself that would appeal most to my audience. Although the novel is fiction, I still wound up on every page and in every sentence. That's the difference between telling a story and writing. A story-teller puts words on the page for the sake of entertainment. Every writer is a story teller, but a writer must take their story a step further and put themselves on the page, allowing their audience to judge them as a human being. Opening up one's self to judgment forces the audience to look inside and judge themselves. Through this process a writer is able to manipulate and shape the hearts and minds of their audience. I not only put down my good qualities. I also put the monster inside me on the page.

"I have the uncanny ability to do the exact wrong thing at the wrong time – like registering for your class without first reading your book." I pointed at Dikface. "Had I known you weren't much of a writer, I would never have made that mistake. This isn't as much a fault on my part as it is a failure in education of consequence. People my age are ignorant of the bureaucratic process built up to secure the power of older generations. Regardless of my past mistakes and the consequences that came with them, my good aspects still outweigh my bad ones. I know that I've written a great novel because I refuse to fail. I don't give up. I was in the Navy for five years and I got out as a paid E-6 – most people in the military don't make that rank for eight or ten years. I could've stayed in the Navy and had quite the career, but I expected more from myself than running the military. Had I followed that path I would have been limited in my ability to advance and I knew I was just as qualified at twenty-three to run the military as those already in charge. What can I say, I'm vain. The modern military lacks true understanding of strategy, and I saw that first hand. We are trained to fight warfare by attrition – it's the remnants of Napoleonic tactics that reside in modern combat. But war is not about this attrition based strategy. War is about the journey from and the return back to peace.

"During my last couple months in the Navy, I almost completely rewrote Naval Air Warfare doctrine. I was brought in to sit down for Captain's Mast a couple days before I got out. We discussed my military career and my future possibilities. I had the world in front of me, but I made the choice to walk away. Leaving the military behind was one of the easiest decisions I've ever made, but it came with some of the most dire consequences considering I separated at the beginning of the Great Recession. I've been through a lot since I got out of the Navy, but I wouldn't change a minute of what's happened.

"I've also worked in restaurants since I was fifteen years old. I've worked in kitchens, as a dishwasher, as a server, and now I'm a bartender. If people in the rest of the world were held to half the standard that I and the rest of my industry are held to, we'd live in a perfect world. If a customer is even slightly dissatisfied with what they order, the restaurant must incur the cost of that return and do whatever they can to make sure the customer is pleased. Not only that, I'm often treated poorly by those same customers. The vast majority of people are quite enjoyable to serve, but it's the minority that does nothing but complain who really piss me off. This is the world I live in and the world I wrote about. It's not perfect like the world you're trying to build here at The University. My genre is reality."

Dooshback stepped in and said, "No one is arguing your skill as a writer. But bartending, military experience, and writing novels are far from creditworthy in the world of academia."

"I'm not an academic and I have no intention of becoming one. Academics are dependent upon creative minds like mine. Without creativity there would be no art on which to debate academically. It's my military experience and the many conversations I have at my bar that prepared me to write. The only two ways to hone one's skill as a writer is through repetitive writing and verbal speech."

The room went quiet for a minute and I chalked that round up to a small victory. But the war was far from over. I was on the Highway To Hell and I felt like I was playing Mike Tyson's Punch Out on original Nintendo. I was the little boxer guy and the bastards were the oversized opponents. Professor Styles was the Mario referee. Right about now he'd be counting while the bastards were on the mat. I'd made it through Dikface. Now it was on to the next bout.

"Where do you think your novel would fit into the literary canon?" Dooshback asked.

I sat up straight and looked her in the eye as I spoke. "Everything ever written is a piece of the literary canon in some way. Many pieces are withheld by academia because the texts haven't withstood the test of time yet. Texts like Beowulf and the Lais of Marie de France may not have been regarded as much of anything in their time, but they're viewed as literary because they're the only insights we have into the artistic minds of their day. The same can be said of the early colonial period in the America. Very little was written artistically, so the only insight we have is the letters they wrote. The literary canon is a fluid concept, and it's our window into the social psyche of the past. The box in which academia places what they decide is or isn't literary is a limitation on their own creative minds. That's why I refuse to become an academic. Academics limit the literary world for the sake of self-justification. That was half the reason why I chose to leave The University for the semester to finish my novel. I was told I wouldn't be allowed to write a creative thesis. My thesis was supposed to be the culmination of my education at The University, and I would have liked to write something I wanted to write. You," I pointed to Dooshback, "told me that I would have to write an academic thesis to graduate."

"Many students chose to pursue academic theses instead of creative ones. They made that choice of their own free will and many enjoyed the topics they chose to write about." She actually turned her nose up as she spoke.

"That's because the students trusted their teacher. Did they really have a choice, or would they have been told the same thing you told me when I resisted the recommendation to write an academic thesis?"

"I couldn't tell you because you were the only student that resisted the change."

"Exactly what I expected, so let me ask you this: what have you written outside the world of academia, professor?"

"I've only written academic pieces. I've published dozens of articles in several academic journals."

"And the only people that will ever read what you've written are academics. Academics write to a limited audience because no one else would take the time to read that crap. If there were anything I'd withhold from the literary canon it'd be academic articles. The majority of academics don't have the ability to write creatively because they're obsessed with 'critical analysis.' Critical analysis is purely deconstructive, but creativity is constructive. Anyone can pull something apart, but creativity allows someone to build a world outside this one – a perfect world populated by imperfect people or an imperfect world populated by perfect people. As I said with my military service, I expect more from myself than the world of academia can provide. I believe one should have to learn to write creatively before they can ever begin to think critically. Anyone can be a critic, and a critique is an opinion no matter how you slice it."

"It works the opposite way in the real world." She leaned forward in her seat. Both her palms were flat on the table and her head jerked as she spoke. I'd brought the bitch out in her. "One must complete an academic thesis before they can apply for the Master of Fine Arts Graduate program. Once in the MFA program students are taught the correct way to write."

"You can't teach someone to write – it's an art. The word 'art' is derived from the Greek word tekhne – which means 'hand work.' If you took the time to read Plato, you'd know that artisans in Greece had to practice their arts day in and day out to master their craft. Writing, like any artistic process, is no different. Although a teacher can guide a student through the artistic method, artistic skill is developed through repetitive action. Writers must hone their skill through repetitive writing. I've come far enough with my writing that I don't need a teacher anymore. I just need an audience.

"I took both the creative writing workshops, although I took the upper level twice." I gave Dikface a narrowed look. "Both classes are required to write a creative thesis, but I wasn't allowed."

"I'm the head of the Literature Department and I decide what is and is not written."

"You decide what is and is not written, that's censorship. Who are you to decide? You couldn't write your way out of a brown paper bag with a magic pen."

"Pump the breaks, Michael." Professor Styles sat up in his chair. I always respected his ability to sit back and listen to someone. No matter how stupid the comment he always allowed everyone to finish – except me when my temper got out of control. "We've spent enough time talking about the literary aspects of the novel, but we haven't taken the time to talk about the novel itself. Although I think there are some parts of the novel that could use some work, I thought it was very well written. You haven't mastered the craft, but I feel you have a very good concept of literary devices and how to use them. The abstract says it all:

"'Sometimes the only thing standing between a man and his worst nightmare is the angel at his side. Holt's life was almost perfect, but everything changed the night he came home to an empty house. Sera, his wife, left him when she learned about the un-mailed envelope he kept hidden away for more than a decade. The man who thought he had everything found himself alone, hiding a secret he could not bear to face. He found comfort in the arms of new angels, but the truth remained long after his loneliness faded. Now, the envelope is out of the office, and it's a delicate race against time to burn the past that could teach Holt how human he really is.'

"Let's start with fear and the fact it was sealed inside an envelope locked in an office in an apartment the owner wanted to sell. This is a great example of the post-gothic method, and it's indicative of the way people compartmentalize emotion. There's a lot more to that envelope than what's inside. The reader has to come to understand why it's been locked away. I think Holt opened the office a little early, but you carried it through to the end. And that was just one of many symbols you used in the novel.

"The sea wall was another great example. A little blunt, but you eased the reader into the symbol. That's what made the symbol such a success. The way Holt and Sera transitioned from opposite sides of the sea wall to the same side was a strong metaphor. If there were ever a success of Wordsworthian similitude, that was it.

"Then you have the angels. I loved the way you used the different angelic glows to build the light in Holt's life – or lack thereof. There was one name that really stood out, though. Who was Sera? I've never seen the name spelled like that before."

"Sera's an angelic reference. You'll have to get a dictionary if you want to find out what it is. Just start with those four letters and you should get it pretty quickly. But I won't give it away. Never have and never will."

Styles laughed as he sat back in his chair. "I don't care whether this novel is accepted for credit or not. I think it will be a great success and I'd love to help you finish this for publication."

40

The Administrator's pen stopped moving at the sound of the last word. He set the pen on the table and flipped through his notes as he spoke. "Michael currently has a negative balance of seven thousand dollars with The University." Finally, we'd arrived at the bottom line: money. "Regardless of whether the school accepts the novel for credit, there is no way to adequately charge for the remaining nine credits Michael needs to graduate."

I was sitting right in front of him. "Charge me whatever you want. It's not about the money to me. I just want someone to say I've graduated so I don't have to pay the VA back. That's a lot of money I don't have. It's not my fault this school wasn't prepared to educate a mind of my caliber."

"It's not that simple." He turned toward the professors as he spoke, "Students are charged based on the time they spend in class, and he would have to spend the required time in those classes."

Dooshback chimed in, "He also has to take both sections of the senior thesis seminar consecutively to fulfill the degree requirement. That means he has to come back for both the fall and spring semesters in the next academic year."

"I can't afford to pay for the classes, and feel free to address me while I'm in the room."

"Why wasn't he directed to private loans? That's one option we have to move forward so Michael can finish his degree."

"I was denied any outside loans because of the debt I've already accrued while attending The University."

"He has the option of a cosigner." What a dick.

"Who's gonna cosign the loans? Are you, mister…what's your name anyway?"

"He could always talk to his parents about cosigning the loans."

"My parents are dead, mother fucker." I snapped to my feet and the force from my straightening knees flipped my chair over behind me. My thigh hit the table, and the shockwaves through the sectioned table spilled the Administrator's coffee all over his notes. My voice filled the room as I pointed an angry finger at him. Still, he stared at his tablet on the table. "That's not in your notes, is it? My parents have been dead for nine years. I joined the military so I wouldn't have to worry while I was in college. If it weren't for your bullshit bureaucratic method, I wouldn't be in this situation. I came to Washington to get an education, but The University only sells degrees. No matter what, education comes down to money. You spout off like this degree is some all important piece of paper to unlock opportunities. Opportunity hasn't knocked, so I built a door. That's what I did when I wrote my book. It's my opportunity the world wouldn't give me. I'm sorry that I'm not the traditional University student – simple minded with rich parents or any parents for that matter. I've never been a conformist and I'd rather walk the road less traveled than follow the path of least resistance. I'm sorry I'm so different from what you want here, but I thought our differences were supposed to make The University strong. Everyone here is so concerned with trying to be an individual no one can see how dimensionless this place really is."

"Michael, you should step outside and cool off. Let me handle this from here." Styles stood and saw me out of the room.

Before the door closed, I turned and said one last thing to the bastards, "I don't need your degree. I graduate myself."

I followed the hall that circled the atrium at the building's center. There were only two classrooms in the Ivory Building, but there were a shitload of offices. The University built the majority of its new buildings for the sake of recruiting new professors. Who cares if there was any room to educate the growing student body, professors got their own offices if they came to profess here. It was clear what was most important to The University.

When I walked out of the building and into the main quad I sat on a bench at the bottom of the stairs. I chain smoked while I waited and pulled Chasing Angels out of my backpack. I brought it with me in hopes I'd get an opportunity to sit down with a few people and talk about what worked and didn't work between the covers. Boy was I wrong. Aside from professor Styles, I don't think anyone even looked at the first page.

I read the first page over and over again while I sat outside. It was such an alluring beginning – a vignette of lyric, love and loss. I'd let many people read it, and everyone was in love with the book by the time they flipped to the second page. I'd built a great beginning, but following through to the end of the novel was one of the hardest things

I'd ever done. It may have been a book I wrote for a girl, but it was good enough to conquer the world with.

"I've resigned my position with The University."

I looked up from the page and flicked my cigarette toward the grass when I heard the sound of Professor Style's voice beside me. "Don't quit over me. I'm not worth it."

"I'm an attorney and I teach because I enjoy teaching. I didn't get into education to see good students with great minds fall through the cracks. I don't need this job to keep my bills paid, but I look forward to reading the rest of your work over the years. There's no ceiling to your potential as a writer, and you already have a leg up on everyone else – you know how to live without money. You really should finish your degree though. You're so close. It could really help you get your foot in the door."

"I'm just gonna kick the fuckin' door down. I'm tired of living by everyone else's rules."

I put the manuscript back in my bag before standing to leave. After shaking the former professor's hand, I made my way back to Massachusetts Avenue. I was on foot, and it was between forty-five minutes and an hour walk to my apartment. I would have driven that day, but it cost too much to fill up my truck, almost eighty bucks. I'd already dropped a c-note to fix the breaks, and that was more than I could afford. That's what I had feet for. Between restaurants and the Navy, I spent a lot of time walking. I'd done upwards of twelve hours without sitting down or stopping in the past, so an hour walk was nothing.

I didn't have any music, so I played with my phone to pass the time. Jessica hadn't texted me since the beginning of the year, and it didn't look like anything had changed. The only notification on my phone was the voicemail-tape symbol in the upper, left-hand corner. There were exactly seventeen voicemails, the phone's voicemail capacity. I didn't have to listen to them to know they were all from bill collectors. At no point had I said "screw these guys I'm not paying them." I would have paid all the bills if I had the money. It was a conscious choice I had to make between which bills were necessary and which weren't. I stopped using the credit card, so paying it off had no real benefit. The cable and internet had been shut off for months, but I didn't watch TV and

Starbuck's had free internet. Fuck the medical bills because they just came out of nowhere at the worst possible time. Everything slowly piled up over the last few months. All I'd been paying since I dropped out of school was rent, car insurance, electricity, and my phone bill – the bare essentials.

I counted the money I owed in my head. The medical bills were around two thousand dollars. The credit card was another fifteen hundred dollars. I owed the cable company six hundred dollars. My monthly expenditures for the four bills I still paid were around 2200 dollars, and I was still coming up short. I had the money to pay rent for May, but what was I going to do for June. Summer was the slow season at my bar, and there was no way I was going to survive another four months until the end of my lease. The bills were stacked so high I couldn't see the light of day. I didn't have anything holding me down. It was time to Duck And Run – to flee the fray and live to fight another day.

When I got back to my apartment I took stock of everything I owned. There was a couch, loveseat, matching chair, coffee table, television, entertainment center, surround sound, bed, computer, computer table, and a dresser. The rest of the small items could go into the garbage. If I put everything up for sale online, I could cut weight before the tenth of May when rent was due. I could keep all the money I'd set aside for bills to get wherever I wanted to go. The only other question was whether or not I was going to sell my truck.

I wasn't the only person on the planet faced with these types of problems. Everyone was running out of money, except for those few we referred to as the 'haves.' Us 'have nots' were left to fend for ourselves in a nation that merely claimed to be free. It was an expensive world to live in – so much so that life without worry was fantasy for most. I didn't think life should be easy by any means. John Donne said hardship builds inside a man like "gold in a mine." I was a fan of hardship – I think my hardships made a great man out of me – but there's a point when society must draw a line on hardship. There are certain things – an individual's need for food, water, shelter, and basic health – that are rights undeniable. All other things on this planet must be earned, even education. I'd been denied the basic rights of food and water in the past. I'd had to make the choice between eating and having a place to live. I'd been without health insurance since I dropped out of college. Recently I'd been denied the right to an education the People of the United States said I earned through military service. I could deal with getting railroaded, but my right to eat and have a place to live had just come under fire once again. At least I had my books. They were the sword I'd use to fight back against a world that tried so hard to cut me down. I thought a college education would be enough, but you can't use the master's tools to dismantle the master's house. I had to make tools of my own.

I hadn't told the professors about the second book I wrote. It wasn't even with me when I went to the meeting. All the time I'd been working on <u>Chasing Angels</u>, I knew it was missing something. I realized what that something was the last time I saw Jessica. I'd written <u>Chasing Angels</u> for her, but her story was incomplete without mine. Once I started the second novel, it practically came out over night. It only took me four months to write, but now I had to figure out how they fit together.

I took a seat on the barstool in the kitchen. I pulled <u>Chasing Angels</u> out of my bag and sat both unbound manuscripts in my lap. I lit a cigarette and pulled my phone out of my pocket. I tried calling Jessica, but we hadn't spoken since January first. I wasn't surprised when the call went straight to voicemail.

"Hey, it's Jess. Sorry I can't get to the phone right now, but if you leave your name and number I'll get back to you as soon as possible." There was a short pause before the computerized voice took over the message. "The voicemail mailbox is full and cannot accept any new messages." Jess and I were so much alike it was scary. We'd both been through enough in our short lives we kept our voicemails full to defend against more bad news.

"Shit." I burned my hand on my cigarette as I lowered the phone to hang it up. The cherry fell out of the cigarette into my lap. I snapped to my feet to put out the burning ball and the manuscripts flew across the kitchen on their way to the floor. I stared at the pile and said, "At least I used page numbers." I shot Jess a text before I cleaned up my literary mess. "It's me. Let me know when you can talk. If you're willing."

I set the phone down next to the sink and put the pile of paper on the counter to reorganize everything. The manuscripts were still in some relative order, but the pages of the two books were mixed together. As I shuffled them in my hands to straighten them out, it was almost like the manuscripts were the same book. They looked right that way.

I took a seat at the typewriter. I didn't want to pull the books apart, so I stared at the blank page trying to figure out what to call the oversized stack of paper I'd put together. The only idea I had was too simple – as simple as Sera and Holt – one and the other – Jess's book enveloping mine and she'd done to me when we met. I typed out the shamefully balanced title and set the fresh page on top of the stack as the ringer on my phone sang out a new text message. Jessica's number was in the alert screen.

"Yes, I want to see you, but I'm busy with class and finals. Dad's coming into town next week. Give me till after graduation. That's when he leaves."

"Kk See You When I See You."

Chapter 2

Holt looked around the lobby as the elevator doors opened. He waited a moment and did another lap around the space with his eyes before stepping off the elevator into the talent agency. His face broke into a half smile and he gave the receptionist a slight nod as he passed by.

He walked down the main hall and past the break room full of copy-editors. Some of them were trying to hold conversations, but they did so over cracked manuscripts. Each of them was trying to do exactly what Holt did when he started at the agency. Holt was the only person to move straight from a copy-editor's cubicle to a corner office. It took three novels three different agents turned down. He worked late nights in his old studio apartment in New Jersey and sold them without telling anyone. He walked straight into his boss's office and said he had three authors he wanted to sign on. He already had signed publishing contracts in hand. He was given a probationary contract as an agent, but he was immediately promoted when two of the three novels jumped up the sales listing over night. That was Holt's specialty. Most of the other agents referred to him as the 'junk agent.' Holt had this awful ability to take on the clients that no one else had the balls to touch and turn them into bestselling novelists. His success made him think he was born to be an agent. The only thing it cost him was a good marriage.

Nostalgia often set in when Holt made it into the agency's main hall. The center of the large open space was full of cubicles. Each one housed a copy editor pouring over manuscript after manuscript. A few of the cubicles Holt could see inside were clean and organized, but those were the people that majored in business or pre-law in college. Most of the young men and women inside the spaces were English majors. Those cubicles looked just like Holt's had when he started. Stacks of papers and books and post-it notes covered every surface of their small work area. It was scary to think that the literary world rested on the shoulders of these young adults and failed writers.

Outside the central collection of cubicles was a perimeter of offices. Outside each office was a desk occupied by an assistant. Most assistants began as copy editors, but they had already proven themselves enough to begin the vertical assent toward becoming an agent. Holt skipped that step. He walked down the line of offices and assistants until he got to his office. His assistant was nowhere to be seen, so he walked inside. Alex was sitting behind his desk with a mess of papers below her face. She hadn't noticed Holt, so he gave three quick raps on the door to get her attention.

She raised her head and ran around the desk when she saw who was there. She had changed into a khaki skirt and a light blue button-up. Her bare feet bounced off the floor as she jogged toward Holt across the wide corner office. "How are you?" she asked, throwing her arms around him like she had not seen him in a long time.

"I'll be alright, but I'll be better when I get your surprise."

Alex ran out of the office and returned with a book. Holt took the hard-back and turned it over as he and Alex sat down on the long, leather couch by the door. The book had an all black cover jacket. The front cover had four lines of white lettering. The top line had the largest print: "Failing Aristotle." The second and third lines had the smallest print: "The Unstoppable Force meets" and "the Immovable Object" respectively. The lettering on the fourth and final line was medium height: "by Holt Mallory." Centered on the spine was the main title, Failing Aristotle – again in white lettering – and near the bottom was Holt's first name printed over his last name. The only thing printed on the back cover was the abstract:

"One of two things happens when the unstoppable force meets the immovable object. They either destroy one another, or they are forever bonded. Mike spent his whole life chasing and impossible dream, but even a superhero needs an angel every once in a while. Jessica tried to ward off his demons, but even the highest order of angel is prone to error. They called one another friend, lover, and soul mate, but even the truest love must overcome life's ultimate antagonist, time. Mike needs Jessica's inspiration to conquer the world, but Jessica fears she will never be enough to satisfy his ambitious soul. What Mike must find is an ending he can begin with to fail Aristotle and win back the love of his life."

Holt gave the book one more look before he set it in his lap. He recognized his lack of visual artistic talent long ago. Alex's keen eye for decoration was one of the main reasons Holt wanted her to be his assistant. She was an Art History major in college and she minored in Literature. Her ability to decorate a novel's exterior was a great complement for Holt's ability to produce amazing text for its interior. The book was perfect. Holt pictured something more for the cover of his first novel, but the simplicity was more him – or at least the man he was when he wrote it. It was fitting that his simple work of fiction had a simple cover. "I love it. I've been looking for that manuscript for a month."

"That's about the time I stole it out of your desk. I didn't think you would mind as long as I stole it for the right reasons."

"I don't mind at all."

"I've had it so long because I designed this intricate cover that I was going to use. Then I just said, 'Fuck it.' You aren't the intricate type. You're more the simple, no bullshit kind of guy."

"You hit the nail on the head. I just can't believe you lied to me all the times I asked you where the manuscript was."

"Yeah…it's been sitting on my coffee table for a couple weeks. I kept forgetting to bring it back. It's in my desk now." Alex leaned back on the couch and stretched with her arms up in the air, bending both arms at the elbows so her hands crossed behind her head. "God damn you wore me out last night. I just can't wait to go to bed. It's a shame we stopped seeing each other again. I could use some of your sleeping medication."

"Medication?" Holt asked, twisting his face and pushing his eyebrows together. She gave a quick glance below Holt's waist and back at his eyes. Holt smiled and looked at his feet when he realized what she meant. "Like you said, 'It was what it was.' But thanks for today. I really love what you did with the book. Your surprise was just what I needed."

"Maybe now you can try and get it published."

"I've got to figure some shit out before I worry about publishing a novel."

"You should probably take some time off. With moving and getting the papers you have a lot on your plate."

"I'm fine. All I have to do is sign everything. I don't have to take time off for that."

She slid closer to him and placed her hand on his shoulder. "Holt, look at me. You spent the last decade with Sera. It's okay to be a little overwhelmed – maybe even a little hurt. You could always go to New Jersey and talk to her."

"I don't want to talk to her."

"So you're just gonna sign the papers and that's that."

"Sounds good to me. She's the one that left without talking things over. She's the one that sent the papers without a phone call. The meanest thing I can think to do is move on without saying a word."

"The meanest thing isn't the right thing. Take today off and just think about it, please…for me." She squeezed his shoulder and leaned her head to one side, curling the left half of her lips and batting her pretty green eyes. How could anyone resist?

"I hope I'm not interrupting anything." Connor's small hunched frame filled what it could of the oversized door. He wore a dark purple pin-striped suit with a light purple tie and matching kerchief in the single breasted jacket pocket. Connor was the original book agent in New York, and he was the man that taught Holt you have to dress to sell. The first investment Connor made was his suits, and it was rare to see him wear the same suit twice in one quarter. The guy was older than dirt, but he could sell a comic book in a retirement home. He was, in fact, the first agent to invest heavily in comic books in the late seventies and early eighties. He told Holt he got the idea when he saw Star Wars for the first time. Connor was already an old man when the movie came out, so he was not the biggest fan. The special effects, however, gave him a great idea. He wanted to sign on all the comic books he could because he knew one day he would be selling them to Hollywood. Sell them he did.

Connor knew he would never make as much money as agents that worked in other industries like music and acting and modeling, but the written word was his specialty. Comics were just one success. If Connor had to waste any of his valuable time writing a resume, it would have bullet points about how he practically built the concept of fan-fiction and that he sold role playing games in book form when Dungeons and Dragons was still just 'Cops and Robbers.' These innovations were just a few of the reasons he was the proud owner of the largest literary agency in New York City. Connor saw a lot in Holt. They were both great agents. The only difference between Connor and Holt was that Connor took on great writers and sold great books while Holt took on anyone he could find and showed them how to build great works of fiction. Holt was the son Connor's career never allowed him to have. Connor, like most legendary agents, was married to his job and his wives were mere mistresses. Unlike Connor, Holt's wife carried a value that was, at a minimum, equal to his job, if not ten times greater.

"May I have a moment, Holt?" Connors powerful voice filled the large space that dwarfed his fragile frame as he followed the sound through the door. He nodded toward Alex and motioned as if he were tipping an invisible hat. Although Connor admitted time and again he was a business man and not an artist, he should have written the book on swagger and charm. His dialogue bordered on flattery without ever crossing the line into its useless territory. Holt was sure Connor could charm the pants off a straight man or convince a golden-star lesbian to try an Eiffel Tower. His Midas tongue, however, was only outperformed by the presentation of his everyday movement. When Connor walked his feet impacted the floor in silence, and his shoulders stayed even as he stepped. If he was concealed from the waist down, an onlooker would swear Connor glided across the floor as he moved.

"You aren't interrupting anything. We were just blowing off work for a few minutes." Holt said as he stood to greet his mentor. Alex stood and made her way toward the door, kissing Connor on the cheek as she passed. Connor took a seat on the couch where Alex had been as the door snapped shut.

"I just want to make sure that everything's okay. The only time you've ever been late for work was the day after Sera left. And Alex mentioned that something happened when she showed up today. She wouldn't tell me exactly what happened, though." He leaned forward and looked at Holt. As Connor spoke he motioned with both of his palms open to the floor like he was trying to signal the coffee table to slow down. He used his hands as he spoke to reassure a client that he meant no harm with his constructive criticism. "This is your friend speaking, not your boss."

"Although you're my friend right now, I need to take the rest of the day off."

"Take all the time you need." Connor changed the subject when he saw the novel in Holt's lap. "Is that the copy of <u>Failing Aristotle</u> that Alex had printed for you?"

"She told you about this?"

"I helped her with the abstract. I want to be the man to sell it if you decide to publish it. It was a great story. Aristotle would quiver in fear if he was alive to read how you defied his <u>Poetics</u>."

"You just know that you can make another boatload of money off me."

"There's that, too. I always knew there was a writer in there somewhere." Connor stood up slowly and said, "I'll walk you to the elevator."

"Kicking me out already?"

"Unless you want to work today, get the hell out of here. This is your boss talking now."

Holt stood and motioned toward the door. "I was already gonna take off after lunch to meet with my realtor. I've got to meet her to pick up the closing papers for the apartment. I'm gonna have to break the news to her that I'm not making money like I used to. I don't think I can afford a place at the Dakota anymore."

"You've been slipping since your wife left – trust me, I've noticed – and showing up to work late no less. I may have to let you go." Alex was busy at her desk when Connor opened the door and led the way out. Connor smiled as he spoke. He stopped just past Alex's desk and he tried to act serious, waving his finger as he told her, "You're Holt for the day. I'm kicking him out of the office. If I see him back here again you're both fired."

"Here's your book, Holt." She pursed her lips and dropped her head as she held the manuscript out with both hands. "I'm sorry I stole it."

"You're fired," Holt said as he tucked the manuscript under his arm with the hardback she gave him. "I'll call you soon and check in."

Conner did a half stretch before turning to Holt. "Let's take the long way around, past my office."

"You're the boss. Gotta check your messages?"

"I'm an old man and I need the exercise." Connor laced his hands behind his back and looked at the floor as he walked. Holt made sure to match the pace of his elder. "You have a lot going on. You've written a book and you're closing on the apartment in a week."

"Got some divorce papers this morning, too." Holt didn't skip a beat as he broke the news to his mentor.

"I was wondering why you were late. Are you going to New Jersey to sign everything today?"

"Not a chance in hell. I have no problem signing her papers, but I don't want to see her."

"Are you sure this is what you want?" Connor stopped and turned when they were outside the double oak doors to his office's foyer (His assistant had an office). "May I overstep our professional line?"

"Connor, we've worked together a long time. You know I respect your opinion in and out of the office."

"Don't sign the papers – any of them. Just stop being a jack ass and go get your wife back."

"A little critical, but you don't know the whole story. She left me. If we were going to work things out she's the one that has to come crawling back."

"Who cares who left who? You turned into something you're not and she left the new you. It made perfect sense when I read your book. You've never been a real agent. I'm not complaining about your work – you've made me a substantial sum of money – but you weren't selling books. You were taking mediocre writers, rewriting their books, and taking a commission instead of credit. You basically wrote the books for them, but you never produced anything yourself. Sera saw that. She fell in love with the guy that wrote that book under your arm, but let's be serious, when was the last time you wrote something of your own? Be a man and get your soul-mate back – I believe that's how you referred to her in your book. Did you ever try to go after her?"

"She doesn't want me to. She found out I lied about something a long time ago, and she made it abundantly clear she can't forgive me."

"Did she tell you that?"

"That's what I inferred. She left me a note that said goodbye and she left her wedding ring with it. I haven't seen her since. We spoke once, but all she said was that she wanted a divorce. I would say the fact that she sent me papers is a pretty clear sign she won't forgive me."

"But she never said she won't forgive you. And I bet you never apologized either." Connor popped his eyebrows and resumed the walk toward the elevators. Holt waited outside Connor's office and watched the old man walk around the corner at the end of the hall. When Holt made his way around the corner, Connor was still moving slowly toward the front desk. Holt was still a few paces behind Connor when the old man said, "Don't sign the divorce papers just yet. I've been married to my job long enough to know true love when I see it, and I've been divorced enough times to know when a marriage is or isn't over. Why don't you just go after her one time and see if it works? You even wrote in the first chapter of your book – what was it called...'The Soundtrack 2 my Life' – 'it was far from over between us.'"

"First off, that book is a work of fiction. You're close to the quote, but that doesn't make it truth. Second, Jessica is a fictional character I made up. She may look like Sera, but I based the character and the story off someone completely different. The main character wasn't even based on me."

"Yes, you wrote the book about that brute you call your best friend, but you're still a part of the story. Sera is, too."

"I hadn't even met Sera when I wrote that."

"But you were writing about her. You forget how much time we've spent together over the years. I've spent some time with Sera, too. I'm the one person in this office that knows where she falls in the story. Separating her from the story won't delete her memory, so why waste your time trying?" Connor finished and stopped next to the agency's front desk. "This is where I get off. I have a lot of work to finish today."

"Connor, it's always a pleasure, sir – even if you are completely wrong about everything."

"We'll see won't we?" Connor shook Holt's hand before turning to walk back toward his office. Holt turned toward the elevator, but he only made it a couple steps before he heard Connor's voice again. "Holt, I did have one issue with your novel."

Holt turned back after hitting the down arrow on the elevator. The door opened as he responded. "What, that Jessica and Mike didn't wind up together at the end? Not every ending is happy." He backed onto the elevator.

"No, it had nothing to do with the ending. And I thought that ending was a very happy one indeed." Holt was blown away by the statement that carried between the closing elevator doors. "My issue was this: <u>Failing Aristotle</u> felt like only half the story – like something was missing."

Failing Aristotle

Addicted

I'm so addicted to all the things she used to do – in and out of bed. What can I say? She Dosed me long ago – a narcotic relief in a moment of extreme duress. There was something about her ability to say the right thing to calm me down and put me back on the right path. The right path was what I needed. Maybe if she were around I could sit down and get some writing finished. I didn't care if it were fresh, free writing or some kind of re-write. I needed peace of mind.

It was late out and the room was dark. A joint burned in my left hand, and I was using my right hand to turn the pages of my manuscript as I read. <u>Chasing Angels</u> was getting longer every time I worked on it, but it was high time to start cutting it down to size. The manuscript was a little over four hundred pages double spaced, and I'd already read it four times in the past couple weeks. The margins were full of notes. That's what the lay person doesn't realize about the writing process. For every page written, there are at least ten pages read. It's not the writer's block that slows you down in the end, it's all the reading and re-reading you have to do in order to truly understand what it is you're writing. A writer must make sure that descriptions are in line with descriptions, actions connect with actions, and the extraneous rhetorical crap you've put in place for mere artistic purpose is isolated from everything else. That shit's best suited for the end of a chapter.

My reading ritual was always the same. I liked to chain smoke joints and listen to music. I had an old eighty gig iPod Video I left on shuffle. There was three weeks worth of music, so the odds of hearing the same song twice were pretty slim. I wasn't sure how long I'd been sitting in my bedroom. It was New Year's Eve and I'd been at work earlier in the day. I'd volunteered to work through the ball drop, but it was slow. I was out the door by eight thirty. That meant I was home and in the room by eight forty-five. It took me about fifteen minutes to roll a couple joints to get me through the night. I'd been reading for about two and a half hours and I'd made it through one, two, three chapters which was about – page one hundred twenty-five minus page fifty – seventy-five pages. Apparently, I read at half the speed of retarded. I never understood that about myself. Granted I retained everything I read and I didn't really have to focus my mind on what I was reading. I could have an entirely different thought processing while my eyes scanned the page and the information still made it into my brain. The process of reading, however, was still frustrating as fuck for me. I was a really slow reader. Considering I'd read this draft of the novel four times, I was about to vomit at the thought of the next three hundred pages. I knew the draft wasn't ready to publish, but I couldn't figure out what was missing. I stayed home on New Year's Eve to try and finish the novel I'd dropped out of college to write, and I was getting absolutely nowhere.

My phone vibrated on the nightstand. The possibility of distraction excited me…until I saw the number on the screen. I knew the number well. Jess's text read, "Are you awake?"

"No, Jessica. I'm not," I said as I set the phone back down on the nightstand without a response. Sure I'd love to fuck her brains out and get a decent night's sleep for once, but I'd realized long ago writing was much more difficult when she was in my life. It was something about her Toxicity that clouded my ability to think clearly. This wasn't always the case. When she and I dated I wrote all the time hoping she'd enjoy the crap I spewed all over the page – she always did. She thought I was amazing. But when we broke up it was like my mind focused solely on trying to get her back. That made concentration difficult when it came time to sit down and write. The idea of free writing is simple: stop thinking and let the fingers hit the keys. But it's the most difficult to master. In the early phases of writing development, one page is hard to fill. It gets easier the more you do it. I've been practicing the art for years and I can sit down and write ten pages in an hour without getting out of my seat when I'm on a roll.

My phone vibrated again, and again the message was from Jess. I didn't unlock the phone this time to read the message. I set the phone back down and went about my business. The phone rang almost immediately after I set it down. It was an actual phone call this time.

The phone rang a second time and I ignored it again. "Mike, let me in." I heard Jessica's voice outside my window when the phone went quiet. "I know you're in there. Your truck is outside and your light's on." She was on the loading dock just outside my first floor apartment. I was already on my way out of the bedroom and through the living room when I heard her voice through the window again. "I'm so cold."

She was always cold. That was half the reason we'd fallen in love. When we first slept together she slept in a pair of sweats and a hoodie with the hood pulled over her head. As she and I slept together more and more she came to love the warmth of my endothermic core. I felt a little relief under the covers with her exothermic chill. With our balanced body heat, we slept like rocks together.

I was hit with a blast of cold air when I opened the side door above the loading dock. "Get your ass in here."

She half hopped, awkward in her high heels, as she walked toward the stairs by the door. She was in a long black New Year's dress with a long slit up the left leg. Although she'd been smart enough to wear her black North Face jacket, her legs were bare underneath the dress. She slowed down when she got to the bottom of the steps. She was a klutz in heels, so she took each step one at a time until she made it to the landing. "Thank you for letting me in. I know you don't want to talk to me right now."

"You couldn't get the message when I ignored you for the last half hour?" I turned and walked inside. I let go of the door before she made it all the way in. The door was heavy and it shut fast. I heard the door hit her when she tried to walk past it. It was a loud, hollow thud, and I heard her stumble in her heels as she corrected herself. She was tough, though, so I knew she'd get over it. I acted like I didn't notice and continued back toward my apartment.

"I heard you were working tonight. I tried to catch you before you left, but the manager said you left early. I came here to find you."

I stopped and looked at her with clinched teeth when I got to my door. "I'm locked out. I forgot my keys inside."

"I'm sorry. It's probably my fault." She stopped before she was within my arm's reach, probably afraid I might take a swing at her. It was a good thing she stood back because the thought of hitting her crossed my mind when I tapped my pockets and there was no sound.

"Nothing's ever your fault. Wait here." I gave her a hard stare before I walked down the hall. She raised her chin and leaned her head to the right as I turned away. She stood like that with her mouth open to silently apologize and look innocent when I got mad. I might have been over-reacting, but I was pissed and I wanted to make damn sure she knew it.

I stormed down the hall to the front desk. The night concierge was sitting at his laptop with headphones in. He pulled out the left ear bud. "Can I help you?"

"I was taking out the trash and I left my keys in my apartment. I live in one-o-six. I'm locked out."

He stepped away from the desk and grabbed the spare set from the makeshift office around the corner. "Just make sure you bring these back."

"I'll only be a minute." I walked back to my door. Jessica was still standing in the hall. She hadn't changed positions at all. I used the extra key to open the door and motioned her inside. I made sure the door was unlocked before I started back down the hall. My heart beat hard and my hands were shaking. Jessica was the only girl I'd ever considered hitting, and this was the second time the thought crossed my mind since I met her.

I handed the spare keys to the concierge and thanked him for helping me out. When I got back to my room, I stopped at the door and leaned my head against the peep hole, taking deep breaths while concentrating on slowing my heart down. Although I wanted nothing more than to scream at her, I had to keep my cool.

I walked through the unlocked door and relocked it. The light was still off in the living room, and I figured Jess would go straight to the bedroom anyway. I didn't heat the living room in the winter because of my wonderful wall to wall windows. The bedroom cost enough to heat, and I spent most of my time at the computer desk. Instead of joining her in the bedroom, I walked into the kitchen and sat down at one of the barstools by the sink to smoke a cigarette. The sound of silence brought me back to earth, but the peace was short lived.

"I thought I heard you come back in, but I wasn't sure when you didn't come into the bedroom."

"I just need a minute, please."

I heard the door shut and I pulled hard on the cigarette. The fire of the cigarette warmed me a little in the cold kitchen. I wished that cigarette would last forever – that I would never have to go into that bedroom to face her – but Jessica taught me long ago that You Can't Always Get What You Want. When I was smoking the filter, I wet the butt under the sink and threw it in the trash can as I walked toward the bedroom.

I felt a rush of relief when I hit the wall of warm air separating the living room and the bedroom. When I shut the door, Jessica was at the desk going through the hardcopy of the manuscript I'd left there. She'd made it through several pages in the time I'd been gone, but I took it out of her hands, saying, "You can read this when it's published like everyone else."

"Sorry. You've written a lot in the margins. Are you gonna rewrite it again?" She stood and took her usual seat on the edge of the bed.

"It's still missing something." I said as I relit the joint I'd been smoking when she showed up. I passed it back to her and set my ashtray on the bookshelf so she could use it while she smoked. I got back to work. She tapped me on the shoulder, and I assumed she was trying to pass the joint back to me. I waved her off without looking away from the computer, working like I was the only person in the room.

"Can we talk?" she asked.

"Nothing to say."

"Then I'll talk. Why have you been ignoring my calls?"

"You started ignoring my calls first. 'Fire with fire,' isn't that what you called it. You didn't get my message on your birthday?"

"I got your message. I was pissed at you. That was supremely fucked up."

"You got the gift you deserved." I continued my work. I hit the keys harder and harder every time she opened her mouth. I had plenty to say, but I knew where speaking would eventually end up: a fight. It was inevitable. It was like this every time we talked. But, alas, there's something about Jessica's proximity that always burned right through any barrier I tried to maintain. "You told me you saved one thing. What did you save?" I asked.

"The little weed piggy bank I got you for your birthday. I couldn't throw that away." I felt her hand on my shoulder. She tried to pull me around in the seat, but I held my ground. "Mike, look at me, please."

"You want me to look at you? I want you the hell out of my life. We can't always get what we want. You taught me that the hard way."

"We can at least be civil."

"Is that what you call lying to me before your birthday, civility? I know I'm not innocent in this fight, but you pushed it too far."

"You got your revenge. Can't we just call it even? How long have you ignored me now? A month? How long is this going to go on for?"

"I gave you a thousand chances before. That was the last straw. I replaced you with the novel just like you replace me with a new man."

"I never replaced you. I'm sorry I chose him, but he deserved the same chances you got. You and I broke up and he was there. I wasn't just going to turn my back on him. He really is a great guy – was a great guy."

"I'm sorry I can't be your friend, but at least you have him to turn to."

"Not anymore."

I turned my head so that my chin was on my shoulder.

"He saw the manuscript you gave me the last time we spoke, and he did exactly what you said he'd do. How did you know?"

"I told you he's the younger, less interesting version of me. It wasn't that hard to predict."

"But what prompted you to text me that. It was an hour before he asked me. I know you always know everything, but how did you do that?"

"I looked up a teaser for Californication Season 5. It said that Karen married her new boyfriend. I just had a funny feeling and, like I said, I had to get it off my chest. That was the only reason I texted you. Sometimes thoughts just pop into my head. I can't tell you how it works…it just works."

"He broke it off right after I told him no. He asked me if I still had the same feelings for you – did I still wish that you and I could get back together? I didn't want to lie to him. You left behind big shoes to fill, and I told him that my feelings for you could never die. I know you're not writing the novel for me anymore, but I was so excited to finally see it and you know I love your writing and…"

As she trailed off I turned a little further in the chair to get a better look at her over my shoulder. "And what?"

"And he said that he could never fill your shoes. No matter how hard he tried, no matter how many poems he wrote, he would never live up to the bar you set. He didn't want to compete for a fraction of my heart anymore. That's when I showed him the text you'd sent me. He asked me how you knew and I had to tell him that somehow you just seem to know everything. He hasn't spoken to me since."

"I'm sorry he had to get hurt. I told you that you'd have to break his heart eventually. We've both known that this isn't over between us for a long time. Too many people have been hurt in this already. I lost my new girlfriend right before your birthday and you broke his heart when I gave you the book I promised you. It really sucks when things come back around on you, doesn't it?" I went back to work at the computer.

The air was silent. The only sound was my fingers at the keyboard. I wasn't smashing the keys like I'd been a few minutes earlier.

"I just want to make things right with us tonight. You don't have to be my friend. I just wanted to start the New Year with things good between us."

I stopped working. I pushed the chair back and lifted my feet to spin on the swivel and face her. I leaned in toward her as I spoke, pointing with one finger. She leaned back. "There came a moment when you were faced with the choice between him and me. You chose him. On your birthday I was faced with a similar choice. I told you a long time ago I could never finish the novel until one of two things happened: either we got back together or we stopped talking altogether." I raised a finger as I listed each of the two options. "Based on your lack of communication I figured that the former was impossible, so I chose the latter. You replaced me with another man and you wanted me to be okay with it. I did the same thing so I could finally move on and finish the novel I've been working on for the last three years and I'm the asshole." I hadn't realized how far forward I was leaning. I was shaking the fingers I'd raised, and she was leaning away to keep from getting hit. Her face looked calm, but her eyes were full of tears.

I walked out of the bedroom and back into the kitchen. I lit another cigarette and leaned against the stove. I rested my head against the exhaust hood with my eyes closed. She set off a little of that ex-military anger, something I worked hard to contain. Even at a whisper my deep voice could fill a quiet room, but it could drown out a jackhammer when I yelled. It wasn't easy to set me off, but once I was pissed there was no stopping me. She was the only person that could get under my skin like that. I had to walk away before I said or did something I couldn't take back.

The cold air and nicotine worked wonders. I turned away from the stove and Jessica was standing at the entrance to the kitchen. She was leaning against the refrigerator. She was wearing her jacket again, but it was unzipped. I could see the black dress beneath. It fit nicely around her hips, and the halter top made her tits pop. I would have loved to be on her arm in that dress, but that time was long passed.

"You want me to leave?" she broke the silence.

"I didn't want you to show up in the first place…but you don't have to go. I'm not gonna cast you back out into the cold."

"I can cab it home."

"Stay here. I'm gonna keep working, but I'll kill the light in the bedroom so you can sleep. I'll drive you home in the morning. I'm sorry I yelled at you."

She came closer and sat on the barstool. She managed to work her arms around my waist and pull me in close. I rested my arms on her shoulders, but I acted like I didn't want the hug. "I need to finish this novel. I dropped out of school to write it. That means no paycheck from the VA. Money's tight and I don't know if I can make ends meet if I'm not gonna be in school. I promised you I would always love you, and that hasn't changed. But I promised you this novel, too. If there is any chance of us ever doing this over again, I have to finish this book. To hell with school and work and everything else for that matter, I know this novel is the right thing for me right now. I need you to respect this space so I can keep my promise."

"I promised you I was coming back to you when the problems between us started. I don't want to break that promise. I really miss having you in my life."

"I need to finish this first. I deserve the same chance you took when you left me. I need to give this novel a chance."

"So you were serious about taking the semester off from school?"

"I didn't really have a choice when I couldn't register. It was a fucked up scenario. Plus I picked a fight with one of the professors. She didn't want to let me write a creative thesis. This novel is about proving to The University that I don't need them to be a great writer."

"Are you going to go back?"

"I'd love to. But we both know that wanting and getting are two different things. It's not going to be as easy as 'I'm here to finish my degree.' I can't afford to go back. I refuse to write an academic thesis. It all depends on if I win the war or not."

"Why start the war at all?"

"I started the war with the school because I needed to make the novel about that. I figured that if everyone knew I was writing it to get a girl back then no one would read it. I wrote it for you because you're the only person that ever took the time to understand me."

She puckered her lips, curling them at the edges and squinting a little with one eye, that look she always gave me when she really wanted to jump my bones. "It took me a long time to realize the pain you feel. The hell you live in understanding everything in the world around you, but never being understood by that same world. That was why I fell in love with you in the first place. You're scared of letting people see your beautiful mind because you're afraid they can't understand the scope of your potential. People fear what they don't understand, and you don't want anyone to be afraid if they find out what you're capable of."

"You got scared when you came to understand. That's half the reason you stopped loving me."

"No, I just had trouble forgiving you for cheating on me...and everything else."

"I was probably too quick to forgive you."

"I could've forgiven you faster, but I never stopped loving you. I just stopped saying it. I stopped believing it. When that happened you stopped believing in yourself. I'm glad you dropped out of college, though."

"You don't think it was a stupid decision?"

"I think The University was unqualified to teach you, or you were too prepared to learn from them. Either way, dropping out was the best choice you could have made."

We went silent and sat together for a few more minutes in each other's arms. I could smell that hunger in the air, but I had to resist. My cheek rested against her hair and I gripped the back of her neck hard with my right hand. My left arm was resting on her smooth, bare knee.

She felt so good against me, but I had to let go to run the cigarette butt under water.

"You're gonna finish this novel and it's gonna be great," she said as she stood up, and rubbed the top of my head. "I have faith in you. May I please read what you have so far?"

"We'll see." I led her back to the bedroom and took my seat at the desk. When I turned back around, Jessica was pulling off her black jacket. She dropped it to the floor and leaned against the door to push it shut. Her arms were at her sides with the inside of her elbows open toward me. She rimmed the inside of her bottom lip with her tongue as she leaned her head against the door, exposing her neck. She was So Hott in every possible way.

"You know why I came over here tonight, right?"

"Because you wanted to talk and you wanted to make things right between us." I turned the chair toward her leaning forward and resting my elbows on my knees.

"Yes, but I want to make peace, too. I want forgiveness. Like you've always said, we have to make peace to put the past behind us. I wanted that when I showed up. It just hit midnight. It's the New Year."

I looked at the top right corner of the computer screen. It was twelve-o-one. When I stood up, I covered the distance between us in two steps. I thought the force of our collision would knock the door out of the frame. Her head hit it hard, but it wasn't the first time I'd pounded her head into something. It was more than a year since our last kiss. You could say the kiss we shared was border-lined addictive. They have meetings for shit like that. Our lips pressed together so hard my heart hurt. Her arms were up and around my shoulders in an instant. I ran one hand down her back until it was at the bottom of her ass. Bracing my other hand against the door, I pulled her toward me and used our momentum to pick her up as we slammed into the door again. The fact that I was strong enough to pick her up with one arm always caught her off guard. She didn't see herself as a small woman, but I was a monster next to her. She struggled every time I picked her up, but there wasn't a force on this planet strong enough to break my grip – not even her unstoppable force.

I stepped away from the door and turned toward the bed. We kissed a little slower as I walked and we stopped altogether when my shins came to rest at the foot of the bed. I tossed her onto the mountain of sheets, blankets, and pillows. She spread out on the bed, waiting for me to dive on top of her, but I turned back to the desk. I picked up the manuscript and handed it to her.

I tried to hide a smile as I resumed my seat. She didn't say a fucking word. How was that for payback after the last two years of bullshit? Fire with fire. I didn't look back over my shoulder when I heard her dress unzip. I didn't see what she was wearing underneath, if she was wearing anything at all. I didn't care as I heard the dress fall in a pile on the floor. I never looked as she slid on my pajamas and an old shirt. For once in my life, I fought off my addiction for Jessica.

"Will reading out loud bother you?" she asked as she crawled back into bed.

"I've tuned you out many times in the past."

"Kay, good." I heard some movement as she got comfortable in the bed. "'He loved her like crazy, and she said, "You're my favorite."' I really like that line, because it's true."

I went through the motions of typing while I listened to her read. This was the first time she'd read out loud to me since the hotel in West Virginia when she read – the part I was missing.

It hit me right then and there. I knew what I had to write. I wanted to jump up and kiss her again, but I'd have to sacrifice my recent victory. Over time she trailed off. I feigned writing, but I was listening to her the entire time. I heard her shallow breaths get longer as the room went quiet. When I was sure that she was out. I picked up the manuscript off the bed and walked out of the room to the typewriter in the kitchen. I wasn't going to start writing just yet, but I knew where to start. Chasing Angels was all about Jessica, but I had to write my story as well. I'd write the truth backwards, like I did in that short story. I sat at the typewriter long enough to finish the title page for my second novel. It was so easy. I had the whole story in my head already from end to beginning. This was gonna come out quick. I'd been working on this novel longer than I'd been working on Chasing Angels, but I had to finish living this one before I could come to realize where it fit into the story. It was clear how this story would end, but it was the beginning that mattered most. It wasn't the pain we caused in our war to be right. Instead, it was our collision that made the whole story worthwhile. The only way to get Deep Inside Of You, reader, is by showing you how she got deep inside of me.

Once the title page was complete, I left it in the carriage of the typewriter. I walked to the bedroom. For the first time since being single again, I felt tired without a single drop of alcohol. I dropped my pants and crawled into bed in my boxers. I would have loved to sleep in my pajamas, but I never got the luxury when Jess slept over. It felt good to be so deprived.

I watched Jessica as my eyelids gained weight. She may have been able to say no to the guy that tried to write one novel for her, but there was no stopping a man capable of writing two novels at the same time. Jessica probably thought our story was nearly over, but it was just beginning.

Chapter 3

"Where are you? I'm in the courtyard." Holt shook his head as he read the text from his realtor, Brandi.

"I'm coming. Patience, woman," he said to himself, speeding up to match pace with the rest of the crowd. He could see the Dakota at the next corner across 72nd street. He crossed the street and approached the valet.

"I'm viewing an apartment today." He continued past the man in the bright blue uniform toward the gated passageway to the courtyard. Brandi faced away from Holt on the other side of the wrought iron gate. Her hair gave her away. It was auburn and cut short, just past her chin. She straightened it when she had to work, but Holt preferred the way she looked when she woke up in the morning. He had a thing for curly hair. Other than her hair, she looked like anyone would expect a realtor to look. She wore a light gray skirt suit with a matching blazer. Underneath she had on a white button up, showing off what she had without looking like a slut. To top it all off, she was always on her phone. Her phone was pressed to her ear as he approached. He felt his own phone vibrating in his pocket. He kept walking toward the fence and yelled at her without answering. She opened the gate when she saw him and he stepped through beneath the stone carved figure of the Dakota Indian keeping watch above the valet.

"Sorry I'm running late."

"It's fine. I just got here myself." Holt knew she was lying as she turned to walk through the courtyard. "I know we were just supposed to meet so you could get the closing contract for your apartment, but I wanted to talk to you about 17S one last time."

"I'm still having second thoughts. I can get the money together, but I won't have anything left over after. Books just aren't selling like they used to."

She turned and looked at him as she walked, smiling over her shoulder. "You do realize you'll be homeless next Friday if you don't make a decision, don't you? I can still get you in here on time."

"I'm well aware."

"And I should probably tell you that there's another buyer on the line right now."

"Are you cheating on me with another client?"

Apartment 17S had a private entrance in the courtyard. Brandi stopped at the bottom of the stairs leading up to the door. She stepped in close to Holt holding her bag in front of her with both hands. Her face was only inches from his. "I would never cheat on you, baby," she said as she turned to walk up the stairs. "It's one of the guys in my office. He heard there was some delay on your end and he's trying to poach the sale."

"I guess that explains why you wanted to meet here."

She shrugged her shoulders as she held the door open for him. "Maybe it's not the only reason."

She let the door fall shut and gave Holt a narrow look, biting her tongue as she walked past him through the entryway. She set her briefcase against the wall by the front door. "Remember when you first viewed this apartment? You seemed so eager to buy it, but you told me a couple days later you needed to take a little time to think. That was when you gave me a copy of your manuscript." She stopped near the kitchen, unbuttoning the three buttons on her grey blazer. She let the blazer fall to the floor as she gave Holt the 'come here' finger with her right hand. As she turned to walk into the kitchen, she undid a button on her blouse.

Holt walked to the kitchen entrance. He leaned against the wall without joining her in the room. She un-tucked the blouse from her skirt and she pulled it open while she faced away from him. Her chin crossed over her shoulder as she looked back at him and said, "I read that manuscript. I called in sick to work the next day so I could finish it. I called you and begged you to meet me here again. I told you I was going to convince you that you should at least make a bid. It was a buyer's market and this investment was going to be the best thing for you. But that wasn't the real reason I called."

Holt shifted as he watched her unzip the back of her grey skirt. "What was the real reason?" he asked as he leaned back into the wall with his arms crossed.

She dropped her skirt to the floor, but left her heels on as she stepped out of it. She looked over her shoulder again after she stood back up straight. "I was trying to seduce you. Duh."

He couldn't see her underwear before she turned around. The G-string was swallowed up in the back, and the waist straps were hidden under her blouse. As she turned, the triangle in the front came into view along with the matching bra. The print was a lace fleur-de-lis set on a white background. She wore the bra a little loose, and her breasts hung so they drifted apart. She didn't have large breasts, but they were a good sized B cup. When she let them hang like that, the curvature at the inside of her cleavage made her tits look much bigger than they really were. To hell with taping them together under a shirt, letting them fall apart just enough to set something long and hard between them looked so much better.

"Eyes," she said, calling his gaze up to meet hers. She paced back and forth across the wide kitchen as she spoke. "You turned out to be a difficult catch. By the way I figured it I had one night to bed you. I made sure the meeting was after the sun went down. I dressed as slutty as possible under my jacket to give you a little shock when we got here and took our coats off."

"You told me you had plans after," Holt said as he shifted his weight against the wall.

"Shh." She stopped as she snapped a finger to her lips. "Where was I? Oh yeah, I took my coat off, but the slutty, black dress wasn't enough. Nothing seemed to work. It took me almost an hour of belting out stupid facts about this apartment and laughing at all the jokes you told – even the stupid ones – for me to realize that you wouldn't respond to me throwing myself at you."

Holt looked from her to the floor. "Oh irony," he said quietly, hoping she would hear his whisper.

"But...when I mentioned that I'd read Failing Aristotle: The Unstoppable Force Meets the Immovable Object, you became more receptive." She began walking toward him, taking one step for every phase or clause as she spoke until she was inches from Holt's face. "It was only a matter of time before I figured out what guys like you want to hear, before we were naked together on the floor, right over there." She pointed into the dining hall behind Holt and leaned in close enough Holt felt her breath in his ear. "All it took was those four little words."

"Nice shoes wanna fuck?" Her exploits would have worked on any other man in any other situation. She looked so good all it would have taken was a camera for an award winning porno to break out. Holt, however, was in no mood for sex and she took no hints.

"No, silly." She laughed as she spoke, but re-composed her sexy tone to say, "I love your writing." She grabbed him by the belt and pulled him across the kitchen until she was against the counter on the opposite wall. She lifted herself onto the countertop and wrapped her legs around his waist, pulling him in close with her calves. She kissed his neck, rubbing his chest and working at the buttons on his shirt. She lifted her head and whispered in his ear, "There are six rooms in this apartment – seven if we count the laundry room. We're gonna have to hurry if we want to hit them all." She kissed his exposed chest, but he stood with his eyes front and his arms at his side. "Is everything okay? It's fine if you don't want to do this right now. You look stressed, like you need to sleep."

"I am stressed, but not because I need sleep."

She slid off the counter and put her hands on his shoulders. "We can talk about it tonight at dinner."

"I don't think I'm gonna make dinner." Holt looked at his feet while he buttoned his shirt back up.

"But I made the reservation two weeks ago." The concern in her voice grew with every word. "What's going on?"

"Shit came up."

"What, did your ex-wife call?" She smiled at what she thought was a joke.

"No, she finally sent divorce papers."

The words made Brandi go stiff. Her arms fell to her side and she stared at Holt with pointed eyes. Her elbows locked and she balled her fists. "I thought you were already divorced."

"My wife and I have been separated for five months. It's the same thing. I just need some time to deal with some stuff. I don't see the big deal."

"The big deal is that you marriage isn't over yet and we've been sleeping together for five months." When her skirt was on and zipped she paced again as she buttoned her blouse. This time she moved faster and her heels made an angry click with every step. "I think that constitutes a little more than casual fucking. How long after you two *separated* did we sleep together?"

"She and I aren't getting back together. I've known that since she left." Holt shook his head and went back to leaning on the wall.

"How long?"

"It doesn't matter."

"Tell me!"

Holt's eyes went wide when Brandi's scream hit his ears. He'd never heard her raise her voice. After a few breaths he turned his head to answer. "Five days. She left me on Sunday and you spent the night that Friday."

She ground her teeth and walked out of the kitchen, buttoning the last few buttons on her shirt. When she came back in the kitchen her blazer was half over her shoulders and she had her briefcase in her hands. She sifted through the main compartment and handed Holt a tri-folded, blue document. "Here are the closing papers for your apartment. I need signatures from both you and your *wife* to finalize the sale. I'll see you at your apartment next Friday at noon. Don't be late." She stopped before she rounded the corner outside the kitchen. "Oh, and I can still get you this place if you want it, but you need to make up your fucking mind already."

Holt stood silent as she walked away. The contract was thicker than the divorce papers. He thought it would have been the other way around, but, thus far, divorce seemed easier than selling an apartment.

He tucked the papers in his back pocket, looking around the empty kitchen. The appliances alone probably cost more than his apartment in Queens. The oven, refrigerator, and dishwasher were all color matched to the grey walls and cabinets. The stove had a wide range, complete with six burners, a gas char grill, and a movable flat grill that sat over the burners. The exhaust hood was as wide as Holt was tall and the oven was large enough to roast an entire pig. The last five years of his life were dedicated to buying an apartment in this building. It was valued at a little over four million. After down payment, his mortgage would have been around twenty-five thousand a month. Five thousand of that was just for the high ass ceilings.

He walked and stood under the chandelier in the middle of the dining hall, he was too short to reach the bottom of the fixture – even when he stood on his toes. It was impressive that Holt could even

72

consider buying this apartment at thirty-three. At least he could have afforded it before he started slipping at work.

He took one last look through the apartment from where he stood under the chandelier, and he only noticed the space he could never fill. His dining room table was too small to fuck on, so it couldn't go in the dining hall – and it was a hall. He could see into the living room, and his couch, loveseat, and entertainment center would only fill a fraction of the room. He could center everything on the fireplace, but then the study off the back side of the living room would be half blocked. All the furniture would have to run along one wall and the entertainment center would have to sit on the opposite wall to keep the study's passageway open. Only problem was that no one would be able to see the TV across the wide living room, the screen was too small. Furnishing an apartment like this would cost almost as much as buying it and decorating would be a nightmare. He would have to pay someone. He always lived a pretty Spartan life before Sera, so she filled all the wall space when they lived together. He was best at filling shelves with memories and books. The bookshelves in the study were too big to fill in a lifetime of buying and writing books. Even if he managed to fill the shelves, he could never read and retain all the information stored in the millions of pages it would take to cover all the shelves from one end to the other.

As he turned from the living space toward the four bedrooms and two and a half bathrooms at the back of the apartment, the papers at his apartment came to mind. He could never fill that space without Sera.

He caught the subway home. At the apartment he dropped the closing papers on the couch by the backpack and the divorce papers. When he received the backpack earlier, he was in shock, but, now that he had a little time to process everything, he thought about why Sera took his backpack in the first place. The backpack was in the office for the last few years. The typewriter she used to type her goodbye note sat on top of the box in which he stored the backpack. At first he assumed she took the backpack the night she left. That made the most sense when he first thought about the situation that morning, but he got one of his psychic, funny feelings.

Holt walked back to the bedroom and took a long look at the office door as he passed. He stayed out of the room since he closed the door in January and, as far as he knew, the door had remained closed ever since.

But the presence of the backpack seemed off. His life was constant calculation, and something was not adding up. Once he was in the bedroom, he opened the closet door and took stock of what remained of his and Sera's luggage set. When she left, she took one of the set's two large upright rollers and the matching backpack. Why did she need two backpacks?

He walked back down the hall toward the office, but he paused outside the door. There was nothing on the other side except for furniture and fear. He gripped the handle, but facing the bad news on the other side was a lot to bear. After the last time he went in there, he spent a month looking for relief in bottles of Jim Beam. What if another trip inside the room had a similar consequence? He hated the idea of drinking himself to sleep at night, but it was time to face the other side. He had to look for answers, and there were only two places to find them: Sera and the office. Asking Sera was out of the question, so that left only one choice. He closed his eyes and took three deep breaths, counting with every exhale. When the number three crossed his lips, he pushed through the door and opened his eyes.

Everything made sense as soon as the door was open. The backpack's box sat in Sera's desk chair. The lid had the word 'Memories' written across it, and it sat on the floor by the chair. The backpack had always been the first item beneath the lid. Without the bag, the other items in the box were in clear view. Holt's notebooks were lined up along the side of the box. The old piggy bank that said 'I'm saving up for some good weed' was still there. Sera's journal from college still sat atop the monogrammed bathrobes they stole from the honeymoon suite in Vegas. Besides the backpack, there were two things missing from the box: the jar of sand Holt made Sera when he convinced her to run away to Colorado, and the pajama pants she stole from him when they first met. The open box was not the only surprise. His desk had changed as well. The typewriter was still there and the note was in the carriage. But, at the edge of the desk, there should have been a picture, two rings, and a manila envelope. A layer of dust had settled across the desk in their place. If the missing items were recently removed, there would have been two dustless rectangles, but the layer of dust was constant across the wooden surface. The picture, the rings, and the envelope had been gone for some time. When had Sera come back?

Failing Aristotle

Dead or Alive

It's all the same, only the names have changed. Every day it seems I'm wasting away. I tried to live a normal life by doing all the things the world told me I was supposed to do, but I constantly felt there's no place for me anywhere. In short, it's a person's choices that determine the direction of his or her life, but access to those choices has always been controlled by the world around me. I noticed long ago that superfluous choice limits happiness, because too many choices lead a man to recognize all the things he doesn't, or can't, have. In converse, too few choices will drive a person in unpredictable directions. When left with no choice, a man is capable of almost anything. You see, outlaws aren't born to be outlaws; we're often shaped by the choices we're left with. I took my first step as an outlaw the day I dropped out of college to leave the normal life behind. I'd have rather been a wanted man with a soul than whatever normal was in this best of all possible worlds.

It happened in University Central, the brand new bureaucratic center for students. The office consolidated the financial aid office, the office of student accounts, and the registrar's office into one convenient location. It was a one-stop shop for everything University. An administrator most likely got an award complete with a certificate for the idea. Students just got one more headache on the road to a college degree because of one fatal flaw: the front desk was manned by students. Granted they weren't undergraduates – most were graduate students and PhD candidates – but they still didn't have a clue. Most of them were professional college students, but they fell far short of real administrators. They had a basic understanding of students' needs, but this was just a part time job for them while they were in school. We called it a streamlined process in the military, but that's just a fancy word for Stupified.

I was in the waiting area for a long time. There were a few people in front of me, and, to my distaste, I listened to all their problems while I waited. The first young man was worried that he might lose his scholarship. The second person ahead of me was a young woman and, although it was none of my business, apparently her grades weren't up to par. The rest of the students ahead of me had similar problems, and all the answers were the same: "Fill out this form, return it when you're finished, and we'll have an answer for you in three to five weeks."

I was in the Navy for five years. I hated the bureaucrat life, but I was damn good at it. Forms and phone calls were somewhat of a specialty for me. I couldn't tell you how many times I've been told to fill out a form and wait. It took some time, but I learned a valuable lesson about paperwork in the Navy. It doesn't matter what a bureaucrat tells you, there's always someone with the power to bypass the system. If the girl behind the desk cared about the students she was paid to help, she could have forwarded each student to an administrator hiding in a cubicle behind the main desk. Each of the problems I overheard was correctable. All it would have taken was one administrator helping each student for a few minutes. The problem was the intention behind University Central itself. The administrators were passing off the customer service aspect of their jobs so they could focus more on the paperwork side. Instead of focusing on the needs of the individual students, the administrators were focusing on their own wants. I knew better than most how difficult customer service was, and that's just what the administrators were hiding from. Although their job got easier, they opened up more cracks students could fall through.

"What can I help you with today?" the girl at the desk asked as I took my seat.

"I've got to register for next semester, but there's a block on my account. When I went online I found out that I somehow owe the school seven thousand dollars."

"We'll see if we can't figure this out. Do you have your ID on you?"

I pulled the card from my wallet and slid it across the desk. She set it on top of the keyboard and went to work. After she was silent for a while I said, "My education should be completely covered by the VA and federal student aid, and I was told a month ago when I was in here that everything should be fine."

"It looks like all of your veteran's benefits are in order, so that's not the problem."

"I had to bring in a copy of my last tax return for an audit of my financial aid this summer. The people I talked to when I turned everything in back in July said it would hold up my financial aid for a couple months, but it's already the first of December. Finals are in a week."

"I understand. I think I know what's going on."

"Thank God. This is the third time I've asked about this and I haven't been given a straight answer yet."

"You were denied financial aid for this academic year."

"You're fucking kidding, right?"

"There's no need for foul language."

"No, but there's a deep desire. What the hell do you mean I was denied financial aid?"

"It says here that you failed a class last year."

"I refused to finish the class because the professor was worthless. I emailed my counselor and she told me I could retake the class."

"Yes, but there are federal requirements to finish a certain percentage of classes. To remain eligible for financial aid you have to pass at least eighty per cent of the classes you begin. You were taking four classes and you only completed three, that's seventy-five per cent."

"Was someone ever planning on telling me this?"

"I'm sure you received an email."

I spoke through clinched teeth. "I didn't get a fucking email." I gripped the edge of the desk so hard the cheap plastic squeaked under the pressure. "What do I have to do to fix this?"

"I need you to fill out this form. When you're finished, bring it in and a registrar will help you draft a letter of intent. We send those two items to the Department of Education and this should be fine in about six weeks."

"The deadline to register for my last semester of college is in less than six weeks."

"That's why I need you to come back as soon as possible."

"If I ever set foot inside this office again, I'll burn it down." I've never seen a human being as afraid as the woman on the other side of that desk. To stand I had to shift my weight forward. As I leaned forward she pushed her chair back from the desk. Most people that know me aren't afraid of me, but most people that know me are smart enough not to piss me off.

Outside, I walked to cool myself off. I wasn't sure where I was going, but I had to be in motion. I lit a cigarette as I passed through the tunnel below the Ivory Building. It was the closest thing the small, private school had to a student union. There was a small coffee shop and a couple places to get food. It was well past lunch, and the tunnel was pretty empty. That made it much easier to spot Jessica at the other end of the tunnel. She probably couldn't see me, but she would eventually. I crossed the street to make sure she had a wide berth. I kept my eyes straight ahead as I walked, and I saw in my periphery that she did the same.

Jessica quickly faded from my thoughts and I was once again fully focused on my Boulevard Of Broken Dreams. This was it. It was definitely the end of my college career. I didn't have any way to take out a private loan to cover the last year of my college degree. I'd already been denied loans in the past. I worked hard to build good credit, but my life after the Navy destroyed all that. With the post Recession shortages, there weren't many banks willing to loan anyone money.

Besides, why would I stay in a school that wouldn't let me write the thesis I wanted to write? There was no way in hell I was going to class that afternoon. I'd already thrown together the last paper I owed my thesis advisor, Professor Dooshback. I did it exactly like I told her I would. The topic was pretty blah, and it was more of a go to hell than anything else. All I wanted to do was walk home and smoke a joint. I've never been much of a quitter. I like to finish everything I start one way or another, so I'd turn in the paper, take my one final, and be finished with The University. What choice was there? I'd been putting off writing to finish school. I guess with school out of the way, I'd have all the time in the world to finish my book.

The walk home was long and cold. The brake pads on my Dakota were worn to steel and I didn't have the money to fix it. I was on foot for the time being. It wasn't the cold that bothered me on these long winter walks. My only issue with walking was the two hour round trip if I forgot something at home.

When I got to my apartment I grabbed the bucket in which I kept all my loose change. The bucket was almost two thirds full, so there was easily a hundred fifty bucks in there. That was just enough to do the last thing I needed to do before I dropped out of college. I cashed in my change at the grocery store across the street.

I took another long walk in the cold. This time, however, I was walking away from school. The trail between my apartment and downtown Bethesda always offered a soothing walk. Except for the streets that crossed the trail, it was lined on both sides by trees. It was a worthwhile escape from the suburban world in which I lived, a little taste of the home I hadn't seen in a couple years. During the summer the trail was always packed, but the trail was a lot more peaceful in the cold months. The trail ran from Bethesda to the Potomac River and south to Georgetown. This time of year the only people on the trail besides me were hardcore runners and commuters traveling to and from work by bicycle.

When I got into downtown Bethesda, I went straight to the tattoo parlor. They had room to squeeze me in right away. What I wanted was pretty easy. I knew the process and I think the tattoo artist remembered me when he saw me. The artist had a printout with the three Latin words as we walked to the back.

"How do you want me to place this?" he asked while he set up his ink and gun.

"I've got this other Latin tattoo here." I showed him the misspelled words of Julius Caesar on the outside of my right forearm. "I want to put this one on the opposite side so I can read it if I look at it. Kind of a reminder."

When he had his tools ready, the artist turned to me with a strip of paper. He wet my arm and pressed the template on my arm with a moist towel. "Is this what you're looking for?" he asked as he peeled the paper back.

I examined the words the artist was about to ink over. The single line was written in a gothic, block script. The first letter was two inches from the base of my wrist and the text extended all the way up my forearm an inch from the inside of my elbow. I turned my arm over to make sure the location of my new tattoo was in the right position opposite the tattoo I already had. "It's perfect."

I thought about why I needed the tattoo as I lay on the table. I was terrified of the uncertain future ahead of me. To be quite honest, I'd been scared of the world around me since Jess and I broke up. I couldn't be scared anymore. I had to live by my own rules. I was beaten down by the world around me, and I had to remind myself what courage really was. That's what the tattoo was for.

As the hum of the needle against my skin filled the room, I found myself lost in thoughts. The world had become a place in which even the average person could live neither comfortably nor easily. A perfect world would be a boring place, but there's always room for improvement. The problem was this idea that there's not enough money to go around. That's bullshit. The people with all the money don't want to share it. Apparently they don't teach the concept of sharing to rich people. Civilizations crumbled for this very reason. Greece didn't want to share land. Rome didn't want to share power. Renaissance Italy didn't want to share money. Americans don't share anything. I gave five years of my life to my country, and I was the one that had to drop out of college. Maybe it was an arrogant thought, but I was far too prepared when I came to college. When I was in the Navy, I invested most of my money in books. Although there were greater libraries out there, mine was one of the most well rounded libraries of any twenty something throughout history. Before I was assigned Shakespeare I read Plutarch. When professors quoted Machiavelli, I quoted Titus Livy and Flavius Vegetius. I skipped most readings in my introductory philosophy course because I'd already committed the writings of Plato and Aristotle to memory. The University may not have wanted a fight, but they were damn sure about to get one. If for any reason, I'd do it to teach them the true meaning of the word intellect. The battle was going to be the first in my war to conquer the world.

It was time to be brave again. What happened between Jess and me had gotten in the way of my life's work. I didn't blame her. It was my fault. I forgot how to be myself, the man that can do anything to which he sets his mind. Maybe, if I put a reminder on my arm, I'd finally sack up, put my mind to something, and do it. I already had a hard plan in place to bring my life's work to fruition. Granted that plan involved Jessica, but I could write her out of it – just like I wrote her out of my book. I had to wait for the right opportunity, but total economic meltdown was only another year or so away. There was a limit to the mathematical economic model, and the wealthy of the world had already pushed that limit. I couldn't rush genius, but time was of the essence to make sure that I was ready when the time came. All I'd have to do was step up when the time was right and Ride The Lightning - give the world something to buy while everyone's selling.

I guess that meant the book had become my life. With this tattoo, I'd have all the same tattoos as Holt in <u>Chasing Angels</u>, except the cross. I stood in the mirror when the tattoo artist had finished his work.

"If you ever need anything touched up it's free of charge." He gave my arm a final rinse and taped a paper towel over the fresh tattoo. "Keep this clean and moisturized. Use a scentless soap and lotion. I'm sure you already know the drill, but I've got to tell you."

"Thanks brother," I said as I slipped a twenty in his hand.

"What does it mean anyway? In English."

"Audentes Fortuna Iuvat. Fortune favors the bold. It's from the <u>Aeneid</u> by Virgil."

"That's straight, man."

After I left the tattoo parlor, I caught a bus back to The University. Although I wouldn't finish college, I still wanted to finish the semester. I went straight to the library to print off a copy of my last paper. I logged on to a computer in the basement. I emailed Professor Dooshback to let her know I'd be taking the next semester off school and that I was going to slide her last assignment under her door. I kept it short, and thanked her for her time. I printed off a copy of <u>Chasing Angels</u> as well. If it was going to be my life from this point forward, I might as well start tonight. When I was finished on the computer, I waited at the printer for the novel to run off. It was a couple hundred pages, even when I single spaced it and printed two-sided.

When the printer was finished, a line of people were waiting behind me. I kept my head down as I slipped past them toward the front door. That was when I saw her. Of course, it would be a day like today I'd be lucky enough to see Jessica twice. She was smoking outside when I walked out. Deals a deal, we have to say hi and be civil.

"How are you?" I asked as I joined her in the Colder Weather and lit up.

"I don't want to talk to you. My boyfriend's in town and I've got a lot going on right now. I'll talk to you after finals." She didn't look away, but she didn't walk away either.

"I didn't want to see you at all." I might as well push it. "How are you?"

Failing Aristotle

"Pissed."

"Me, too. Do you know what it was like when I found out you lied to me?"

"Do you know what it was like coming home to that gift on my birthday? You even took the time to wrap it. I had no idea what it was or who it was from when I saw it. After I opened it up, I walked the whole thing to the garbage chute. I only saved one thing. What the fuck was going through your head?"

I dropped the cigarette and stepped it out, looking at the ground as I did so. Whatever she saved didn't matter. As far as I was concerned she was just baiting me. I couldn't trust her anymore. I just convinced myself that what I had to say was poetic justice. I forced the draft of Chasing Angels in her hands, pushing past her and saying, "Same thing that's going through your head right now, Jessica: 'Fuck you.'"

I stepped carefully through the Ivory Building as I looked for Dooshback's office, peeking around every corner to make sure I wouldn't run into another person I didn't want to see – Jessica was more than enough. Once I slid the paper under Dooshback's door, I practically ran off campus. I'd only have to come back once to take a final exam, but I didn't care anymore. I tried to focus on the breakdown of my college education. Any obsession would have been better than thoughts of Jessica, but I still couldn't get Jessica's face out of my head. That and the teaser I'd seen online for the fifth season of Californication. I looked it up because I'd just bought season four, and I was heartbroken at what I saw. At the beginning of season five, Karen was married to Black Jesus.

Jess and I lived the first four seasons of Californication. The only difference between us and the couple on the show was that we didn't have a Becca. If she married her boyfriend, I'd have lost her forever. Although I'd been asking her to make a decision for a long time, the thought of losing her forever was too much for even my expansive mind to comprehend. I pulled my phone out of my pocket.

I texted, "Jess, I'm not saying you have to marry me. Just don't marry him. I'm sorry. I had to get that off my chest."

Chapter 4

"I'll take whatever you have available." Holt said, driving south along the Garden State Parkway.

"I'll put you down for our top floor, corner suite. It has a balcony with an ocean view. It is our most expensive room, but it's the only room I have available right now. Does that sound okay?" the voice came over the Mercedes stereo – hands-free technology at its best.

"Just put me down for one night. I should be there in a couple hours."

"Great. Is there anything else I can help you with today?"

"That'll be all. Thank you."

Holt ended the call and the radio turned on automatically. He left his apartment early enough he was out of Manhattan and across Staten Island without any trouble. If he left an hour later that route would have taken hours. It may have been the shortest distance to the Parkway in miles, but, when measured in more realistic units – such as units of time and sanity – it was leagues longer than any other route. The mess of bridges that separated New York City and the great state of New Jersey made Holt wonder why anyone would commute so far by car. Sera used to take the train to get back and forth – it only took an hour or so – but that same journey by car went upwards of two to three hours, depending on the chosen path and density of traffic. Today, Holt felt a taste of the days when he could look from the clock on his car stereo to the mile marker on the side of whatever highway he was driving on and calculate his arrival time within minutes. The time he'd saved by leaving town early gave him an idea.

Holt pulled off the Parkway and took State Highway 35 to Highway 36, appropriately named Ocean Avenue. It was the perfect afternoon for an early summer beach drive. The Jersey Shore was a panoramic postcard of lighthouses, summer homes, and white sandy beaches. Between Memorial Day and Labor Day it was the playground for the New York elite, celebrities, reality TV shows, and anyone else in the mid-Atlantic states with too much money and not enough work to do. Holt fell in love with the area overnight the first time Sera invited him to visit right after college. Close to the water, the beach towns were pretty much the same. It was a never ending pattern of beach houses, hotels, bagelries, and surf shops. Those buildings were all outside Holt's passenger window. He didn't waste time looking that way. He was checking out his first love, the sea. The first time he saw the ocean, he was enthralled how it stretched out and ended in a perfectly straight line mankind named the horizon, the only straight line God ever made.

The trip along the beach added an hour to his journey, but Holt didn't mind. Towns and townships passed without notice, and his eyes remained locked on the water. He was zoned out on the waves until he finally came to his senses in Belmar, two towns north of Seagirt. The last two towns bled together and Holt had to make a small detour down First Street. Ocean Avenue wasn't continuous in Seagirt. It meant two extra blocks and four quick turns. Sera's lighthouse came into view after the third. When Holt first saw it eleven years ago, it was a lot different than he expected. Most postcards and movies showed spire lighthouses, but this one was a cubical, red-brick building. It no longer operated, but it was one of the small town's big landmarks. Sera always claimed it as hers. Holt pulled off to the side of the road in front of the hotel across the street from the lighthouse.

Checking in was quick, and Holt unloaded his backpack before parking his car around back. His room was long and narrow. There was a kitchenette and a couch just inside the door and a big screen TV on the opposite wall. At the very back of the room there were two doors, one in each corner. The sliding door to the left opened up to a small balcony facing the beach. The other door opened to the bedroom. Holt threw his bag on the couch. He would have taken some time to settle in, but he didn't even bring a change of clothes. "I've got to talk to Mike. He's probably at work."

He walked out of his room and down the stairs. When he got outside he turned away from the lighthouse toward the blackboard a-frame on the sidewalk a couple hundred yards away. It had the name of the bar and the daily specials written on it in pink and green. Dollar-fifty domestics were a great deal no matter where you were. As Holt walked past the a-frame he read the sign above the front door before walking in. The name of the bar, Happy Hour, flashed in neon blue and the subtitle, The Sinner's Chapel, flashed in green below it.

"Holy hog-shit jumpin' Jesus. When the hell did you get back in town?" Mike's voice filled the room. He owned the place, but he preferred his place behind the bar. Holt practically lived at the barstool on the far right before he and Sera moved to New York, and he visited almost every weekend before Sera left him. It was good to be back.

"Just got in. Naturally, this was my first stop." Holt said as he reached across the bar to shake Mike's hand. "Been a while. How you been, sir?"

"The Bennies are pilin' up, but that means more money for me." All the locals called the outsiders that came into town for the summer 'Bennies.' It was an inside joke for those that never left the shore. Holt would have taken offense when people referred to him like that, but those that used it knew little of the outside world. Like anyone from any small town, most people that grew up in Seagirt never took the time to leave.

"Last time I checked you're a Benny yourself, Michael."

"Last time I checked, I still live here…and I can kick your ass. I'm a local by squatter's rights." Mike grew up in Oklahoma, but he ran away at eighteen to join the Navy. Holt met Mike during their freshman year of college. They were roommates then and they had been best friends ever since. Their respective wives introduced both of them to the Jersey shore some years back. Mike moved to the shore right after he dropped out of college to piss off his soon-to-be fiancé. Holt and Sera moved to the shore after a failed year in Colorado. Everything else was history.

"Watch the bar," Mike ordered another bartender as he grabbed two beers from the cooler. He picked up a couple shot glasses and a bottle of whiskey before he rounded the end of the bar. He motioned for Holt to follow as he walked to a table in the back. "What're you doing back in town? Got anything to do with Sera?"

"Yeah. How'd you guess?"

"Unlike you and me, she and my old lady never stopped being best friends. They still talk all the time. She comes in here every once in a while with…uh…some guy." Mike poured a couple shots. "Pain medication to cure the broken heart."

"Don't mind if I do." They tapped glasses and took their drinks after sitting down. "You talk to her at all? How is she?"

"We talk whenever she comes in. She seems fine. I never bring you up, though. Considering she seems pretty friendly with this guy she's seeing, I thought it might be a volatile subject."

"So she's like seeing-seeing this guy?"

"'Fraid so, sir." Mike poured another round of shots.

"I guess that explains the papers I got this morning."

"*The* papers...ah fuck." Mike took a courtesy shot without Holt. He refilled his glass as he said, "So it's official? You guys are calling it quits."

"I assume so. We've only spoken once since she left and that was so she could tell me she wanted a divorce."

"When was this?"

"In January. A few days after she left."

"And you're just now getting divorce papers." Mike lifted his hands off the table, shrugging his shoulders and staring at Holt. "That doesn't seem odd to you."

"Should it?"

"Yes. That girl's been crazy about you since the moment she read your book. What the fuck happened between you two? I always thought you two were bulletproof."

"No idea." Holt kept his eyes on the floor as he spoke.

"C'mon man. Cut the crap. It's me you're talkin' to. What'd ya cheat on her or something?" He lowered his face and looked at Holt through his brow.

"Nah, I never cheated. I mean, I slept around after she left, but that doesn't count. I just came home one day and she was gone." Luckily Holt was an amazing liar. Holt told Mike about the place at the Dakota and their anniversary when he came home to an empty house. He told Mike about the rings and the note in the typewriter. By the time he'd finished his tale there were a half dozen beer bottles on the table, and they had done some solid damage to the whiskey bottle.

"That doesn't really sound like her. She never told you why?"

"Like I said, we haven't really talked."

"You could always try talking to her, or, hell, you could even write her a book. That's how I fixed shit between me and Caitlin when we split up in college."

"You know I don't write anymore."

"Neither do I, but that ol' tale of tattoos and scars was one hell of a weighty tome. Now that you're a big New York agent you could always take it and run. Cait still has her copy."

86

"It wouldn't be right after all this time. Not since Sera left." Holt gripped his bottle tight and took a shot.

"Scars are souvenirs you never lose." Mike held up his beer. Maybe their old toast would cheer Holt up.

"Tattoos are lessons we never stop learning." Holt tapped the neck of his bottle to Mike's and they took a long drink.

Mike changed the subject, leaving the depressing topic behind. He filled Holt in on the recent history with his two kids, flipping through pictures on his phone. "Swear to Christ, I blink and they've grown an inch."

"Your kids are growing up faster than you are. They're probably more mature than you already."

Mike held up his middle finger as he spoke. "I'm mature. I've just decided to remain young at heart."

"You still smoke weed?" Holt asked.

"Duh. But I don't do it around the kids? And don't judge me slap-dick. I seem to remember you were quite the stoner in your day."

"I'm not judging. Do you have any?"

"That's a stupid question. You wanna go smoke? I thought you quit."

"I haven't smoked in years, but, yeah, I could really go for a joint right now. It's been a long fuckin' day and I think some weed would be great."

"I've got some out in my car. I can throw you a little for the night and I'll get us both some more in the morning."

"How much do you want for it?" Holt pulled out his wallet.

"I want you to stop being such a fuckin' stranger. You really suck since you became a business man. You stopped smokin' weed. You moved to New York. You never call. You never write. You're boring now."

"I'll drink your booze, but I'm not letting you give me free weed."

"Just go halfsies with me when I pick up tomorrow. I'll let you know how much it is in the morning. You staying at your usual place up the street?" he asked as he stood and pulled a cigarette pack out of his pocket. Holt nodded in response. "Let's run out to my car, grab some shit, and go get high."

"What's my tab?"

"Your tab's I own the bar. C'mon."

Holt dropped a twenty on the table. "Sorry for the mess," he told the bartender as he chased Mike out the front door. The light was already beginning to fade as they walked to the alley where Mike parked his old, blue Jeep Wrangler. Holt stood at the corner taking in the sights and the cool ocean breeze. The only sounds were the rolling waves of an ebb tide and the drunken fumbling of Mike in the front seat. The streets and beach were relatively empty for early summer, but the town would be a madhouse in a few more weeks. The sidewalks would be a mess to walk down and the beach would have no room.

A solitary pedestrian caught Holt's eye down the street to his right. He panicked when he leaned forward and saw who it was. "Shit, it's Sera," Holt said as he ran toward the passenger seat of the Jeep.

"Found weed and papers…wait. What did you say?"

"I'm gonna hide in the Jeep. Distract her so I can get away. I don't want to see her. Not like this."

Mike tossed the bag of weed and pack of papers into Holt's lap. "You're lucky I'm your best friend. I'll distract her. Pinch off some weed for yourself, but leave me some."

"I'm taking your papers. I've gotta do my ritual."

"Fuck your ritual. What am I supposed to smoke out of?"

"You own a restaurant. I'm sure at least one of your employees can help you out."

"Whatever. Call me tomorrow." Mike lit his cigarette as he walked back toward the end of the alley. Holt sat low in the seat to stay hidden, but he never took the time to think about how hard it was to hide in a vehicle without a top or doors. It would have been a better idea to hide around the corner at the back of the alley, but then he would not have seen everything play out in the rearview mirror. Mike looked left then right as he scanned the sidewalk, waving when he found his mark. Mike disappeared as he leaned forward for what looked like a hug, but Holt could not see Sera.

Holt tried to listen to the quick exchange, but Mike was sure to get Sera inside before she noticed Holt hiding in the topless Jeep Wrangler. He only caught a glimpse of Sera in the mirror as she walked with Mike past the alley toward the bar's front door. Holt waited before getting out of the car. He lit his cigarette and stepped slowly toward Ocean Avenue.

After checking to make sure the street was clear, he walked around the corner and back toward his hotel. As he walked past the front door of the bar he looked inside. Mike was already behind the bar and Sera sat across from him. All Holt could see was her long, soft, shiny brown hair pulled back in a ponytail. Holt's body shook in fear as he passed the doors, and then his sight of Sera was gone.

Failing Aristotle

Fuck You

I saw him driving round town with the girl I loved. Fuck You, Jessica. Maybe if she'd had the common decency to be straight up with me from the time we broke up, this wouldn't have happened. I'd gone to great lengths to do something amazing for her birthday in an attempt to show that I could leave the past in the past. It was just a jar of sand, but, hell, at least I was trying. I stopped trying when I saw her with him. I dropped that jar of sand in the nearest trash can and decided to give her a different gift. There wasn't a question in my mind about what to give her. I'd give her all I had left. I made a monstrous decision, but, after all we'd put one another through, it felt right. Madness, not anger, comes to mind as I look back on that night; but why will you say that I am mad? Not if you know why I did what I did.

Jessica and I existed in a vicious cycle for some time. We'd make peace, be friends for a while, everything escalated to the point of no return, we'd stop talking, and then we'd have to wait and see when the one of us with the highest claim to innocence allowed for a truce again. We'd made the truce a week earlier. Before that we hadn't spoken for three months.

The transition back into friendship went smoothly for her, but I wasn't so lucky. I made a simple mistake the night Jessica and I spoke for the first time, and my girlfriend broke up with me. I didn't blame anyone but myself. Instead of sitting around Waiting On The World To Change, I focused on doing the friends thing with Jessica the right way. We were back to talking all day every day, and we spent no less than two hours a day together. That's just how we were. We never really clung to one another. That only happened when times got hard. Stuck Like Glue was more accurate. Neither of us has ever really met anyone else we'd rather spend time with. I felt comfortable enough with her to talk about anything, and she found me entertaining. We've been like that since the day we met. But I could always tell when things were about to go bad between us. The end's beginning was always marked with silence.

Jessica called me on Thursday night, but I was at work and missed the call. I tried calling her that night when I got off and the following morning without success. I sent her a text message while I waited for an appointment with professor Dooshback. "Sorry I missed your call last night. I was at work."

I stuffed the phone back in my pocket when the professor called me into her office. "Have a seat, Michael, and tell me what you're thinking of for your thesis."

"Well, I've been reading a lot about the development of printing – or, rather, writing in general. There's been a slow evolution of literacy and the ability to write since people first started doing it, but the internet has really changed everything over the last couple decades. I have this theory about how things are changing. There's this book I've been writing since I started college. After graduation I want to publish and promote it online, because I think that's the future of the writing world. That's not exactly what my thesis is about. Instead, I want to use the history of writing to show how I think Literature is about to change in the near future. It's about the writing and publishing process. That's why I think it's important."

"Interesting topic. I just don't understand where you're trying to go with this. This doesn't sound much like an academic argument."

"It's not meant to be an academic argument. It's creative and philosophical in nature. I know it's not a story, but not everything creative is a story."

"We just need to discuss how to put this into a form to which I can assign a grade."

"Grade's just an opinion. Read it and put your opinion on it. It's not that hard."

"When it comes to your thesis it needs to be something more within the constraints of what the other students are writing."

"I'm not worried about the other students. This is my thesis. It's supposed to be the culmination of my education. If you want me to write a thesis I don't care about, then what's the point of writing a thesis at all?"

"A topic like the one you chose is something that students tend to pursue in graduate school."

"There's about a snowball's chance in hell that I'll go to grad school. Why can't I just write the thesis I want to write now?"

"Because that's not the way the academic world works."

Failing Aristotle

"I'm not an academic. When I write academic papers I don't take them seriously. If you want me to write a thesis I won't care about I can get you one by next week. I'm a writer and I'd really like the last paper I write in college to be one I want to write."

"This is an academic university, and you're not a writer until you've been published. You'll either write an academic thesis or you won't graduate."

"Oh." Although I was silent for less than a second, the relativity of thought provided me with infinite time to consider her statement. Yes, I wanted to graduate, but I was finished writing academic papers. I spent my junior and senior years of college preparing to write a creative thesis, and now my professor was telling me it was no longer an option. Deep down inside me there was an urge to grab Dooshback by her shoulders and shake her until her body went limp. Murder, however, is still illegal in most cases, and I know far better ways to torture an individual. Instead of rushing into a decision I couldn't take back, I decided to leave before my anger got the best of me. "I guess we'll be in touch then. I've got someplace I've got to be."

I shook my head as I stood up. There was something about the look on her face when I walked out the door. She wanted to keep me inside her special student box so she could feel important. I'd write the final paper and finish her class, but writing an academic thesis was out of the question. I'd do what I did with every other paper in college: go into the library x number of hours before the papers is due (where x = the number of pages in the paper), spend the first hour researching online, find three quotes per page to write around, and bullshit all the space between. It didn't matter if the paper was five pages or fifty. The academic method was juvenile. For anyone with any actual writing skill, there's very little challenge.

I looked over the crowd of students as I walked out of the Ivory Building. The majority of students claimed to hail from the middle class, but that was just a lie their parents told them. The middle class was composed of average Americans, but the average American couldn't afford to pay for a private education. The average American struggled to make ends meet. Now, look at the typical student at The University. Many were the children of doctors, lawyers, investors, and bankers. They hailed from households making more than a quarter million a year. Middle-class my ass. These kids were recession proof. After three and a half years walking among these people, I'd really grown to hate them. If I'd caught wind of a terrorist plot against The University, I'd do nothing but go home, grab my lawn chair, pick up a case of beer, and watch from across the street.

I tried calling Jessica as I walked across Nebraska Avenue to the parking lot. The phone rang a couple times before the call went to voicemail. This was the moment I started to really wonder if something was about to happen with Jessica, but I was relieved to see she'd texted me when I got home. Her message said, "I'm working all weekend. I need to make some money. I'll get a hold of you when I'm free on Sunday."

I took what she had to say at face value while I got ready for work. It would probably be a busy night, but I didn't care. I spent a lot of time thinking of what to get Jessica for her birthday, and I was making the trip to go get it Saturday night.

Work came and went like it often does on Friday nights. I was the first bartender on for the night. Happy hour wasn't too bad. It was a decent start to the night. We had a decent rush, and it passed without a hitch. I'd spent most of my life working in bars and restaurants. In time I'd come to fit naturally into the dance we call customer service. Sure, there's the occasional asshole, but the job's actually pretty fun when you get down to it – especially behind the bar. A bartender is everyone's favorite person. Some people just wanted to drink and hang out. Some people came to the bar for someone to talk to. If someone wanted to be left alone I gave them their space, but if someone looked desperate I always gave them a friend and a little Hope On The Rocks. There's an art to the whole process. Learning to read the individual customers was by far the hardest part of the artistic development. Friday nights typically flew by, but the next day was going to be a long one.

Brunch started at ten, so I had to be up at eight to make it in by nine. I did the brunch shift by myself. I was a machine when it came to making Bloody Marys and Mimosas – morning drinks of choice for brunch goers in the District. On top of making drinks for my customers at the bar, I had to make drinks for everyone else seated in the restaurant. The job was all about efficiency. I constantly reviewed where I'd walk next and everything that could be done along the route to my destination. This required an impressive memory. Whenever I was at a table I usually had to take the order with full hands, so I never wrote anything down. I'd be on the move past another table when they'd order another round of drinks. When I finally got behind the bar, I made so many drinks I could never carry them in one trip. That's where experience and a good smile really came in handy. It was all about making sure that everyone in my area of responsibility knew that I hadn't forgotten about them. No matter how busy I was I made sure all my customers felt like they were the center of my universe every time I passed them. Even when I was head high in the weeds I always kept my cool. As long as I was calm the customers were calm.

There's a catch in the restaurant world, though. Whenever the restaurant filled up, I had to take care of everyone waiting for tables at the bar on top of my own customers. When the bar and restaurant were both full, I could have as many as fifty customers under my watch. That's when I really made my money. People liked to have a drink while they waited for a table, so I got them what I could before their table was ready in hopes they'd leave a decent tip before they left. If I got a decent wait during the brunch rush, I racked up quite a bit of extra cash.

By the time brunch was over, I was exhausted. I drove home and took a nap as soon as I got off. The sun was down by the time I woke up, and it was time to make my trip to go get Jessica's present. I'd been looking forward to the trip all week.

I especially liked road trips at night. There's something peaceful about the open road, and it really gave me time to think. The idea of having some time to myself was almost as good as the idea of getting Jessica something I knew she'd cherish. I knew the way to her hometown by heart from all the times I'd made the trip in the past. It was a little under four hours of driving if there was no traffic on I-95. Round trip, it was about forty dollars for the tolls both ways. There was a toll at the tunnel in Baltimore and another at the Delaware border. There wasn't a toll going north across the Delaware Memorial Bridge, but there was one going south. The round trip also cost a full tank of gas. I usually tried to fill up somewhere on the New Jersey Turnpike where gas was cheapest. I hit up the first gas station I passed on the way up, and I usually hit the last one again on the way down.

Failing Aristotle

I got off the turnpike at exit 7A, I-195, toward the Shore Points. From there, it was only thirty minutes to Seagirt. I got a little lost when I first got to town. I had a hard time remembering how to follow the shore down to Jessica's beach. Once I was there I parked on the side of the street and walked down by her sea wall to fill an old mason jar I had with sand. It was a simple gift, but it was the message on the jar that made it all worthwhile. 'The Coast Of Somewhere Beautiful' was written on a note card I glued to the outside of the jar. It was an old Kenny Chesney song I used to love, and I thought it really brought such a mundane gift full circle.

I wasn't trying to waste any time on my trip. I had to be back at work at five the next evening, and I wanted to get home in enough time to try and sleep the day away before work. Hopefully Jessica would call me before work and we'd have time to grab some lunch so I could give her the gift when it was still her birthday. I decided to stop at Wawa to grab a meatball sub before getting back on the road. After I bought the sandwich and walked outside, I saw Jessica with her boyfriend. They were at a gas station arm in arm across the street. What a Bitch.

I picked up my phone and called her. She reached into her purse and looked at her phone as she walked to the passenger door of her boyfriend's car. She was careful not to ignore the call, but instead she silenced the phone before putting it back in her purse. She never noticed me standing across the street as they pulled out of the parking lot and drove past me. I walked back to the Dakota and pulled her jar of sand out of the passenger seat. I dropped it in the trash can by the front door before getting On The Road Again.

I couldn't believe she would do that to me again. She lied to me too many times, and this was going to be the last one if I had anything to say about it. All she had to do was tell me she was going to New Jersey to see him. I already accepted the fact that it was over between us. But after everything she said to me. After I worked so hard to let go she pulled me back in. She could never just Let Me Let Go. She never said she loved me, and the nights she wanted to always ended with the phrase "I can't." She chose her boyfriend, and I was okay with that. I told her that we could give it another shot if we were ever both single again, but I stopped Waiting In Vain for her love long ago. She wanted to be friends. That's all I wanted, too, but an honest friend is apparently too much to ask for.

It was an obsessive drive back to the District. Luckily I had a few hours off before work. I could just sleep and think about what happened. She was the one that said she wanted to be friends again, and she was the one that told a lie. She knew how much I wanted to leave it all behind and start a new life without her. She dragged this breakup out for nearly two years. I couldn't mentally handle the strife anymore. I'd been prone to break down in the past, and freak out. I didn't want it to happen again. Jessica was that only thing on this planet that could crush my emotional control. Everyone has a weakness, and she was mine from day one. I needed to think through my next course of action before I followed through with anything. The next day was her birthday, and I had to give her a gift she'd never forget.

I found myself faced with an odd dilemma. Throughout the last two years Jessica and I were falling apart, we've both acted in two very distinct ways. I got drunk and angry. I didn't know why I got that way. To be quite honest, I was always a pleasant drunk. Even if I was angry when I started drinking, I calmed down after a couple rounds. Then it was back to having a good time. I usually didn't make bad decisions when I was drunk, albeit I may go home with people I shouldn't – take that how you want. Alcohol was never an issue until we broke up. Jessica started lying, but she wasn't a liar by any means. I was the only person she ever lied to. No telling why she did it, but I was sure it was the same reason I turned into an angry drunk. That's why I didn't want this next move made in anger. I wanted to send the right message. I needed to say "Fuck you" appropriately. It didn't feel like a vindictive decision at the time. All I could think about were the things she said when we'd seen each other for the first time in months.

They were the same things she always said. I got confused. You could ask anybody that knew me, and they'd tell you I was never confused. The fact that someone was able to confuse me successfully was a lot to deal with. I'm the one that got inside people's heads. I'm the one that had the power over the people around me. I'd fallen to my own hubris.

I didn't stop weighing over the decision. I'd thought a lot about giving her that box before, but I always thought throwing it away was a much better idea. I'll say this much though, I just wanted to let go of everything.

I made the drive home in silence. As I passed through New Jersey and Delaware and Maryland the radio stations faded in and out. I didn't hear it when it happened. I was tuned out to the world. Every so often a light on the empty highway woke me from my daze and I'd hear the static, flip the dial, and fall right back into my thoughts. It's amazing how much thinking I got done when I drove. In the four hours between Seagirt and Washington DC, I turned my monstrous decision over a dozen times in my head.

I slept well. I slept all through the remainder of the night and halfway through the following day. I don't know how I slept like that. Good sleep is almost impossible for me to find without a bottle or a decent lay. But there was something completely satisfying about finding a recognizable way to tell Jessica that I was finally done. When I woke up I went across the street to the corner store and found a roll of wrapping paper. I picked the cheapest roll on the shelf – it was red. When I got back home, I set the wrapping paper on the kitchen counter and I walked to the closet by my front door.

Tucked away on the top shelf was my box of memories. It was white on the outside, but the cardboard was visible on the inside. It had collapsible ends, and a hinged lid. Inside, there was the little piggy bank that said "I'm saving up for some good weed" on both sides, a pair of Pepsi pajama pants I'd found at Walmart some years back, a pair of flip-flops Jessica bought me when my last pair broke, and a letter she'd written when she told me how mad she was at me for walking away Over And Over. The last thing I placed inside the box was a notebook sleeve she'd bought me when we first got together. It was all black, and it had a pen holder on the outside. It probably cost her a couple bucks at the store on campus, but it was the first thing she thought to get me when she found out I came to college to write. It was the first thing she ever bought me, and it was the only thing I hadn't put away in the box. I'd replaced the notebook inside the sleeve a dozen times and there was a stack of notebooks on the bottom shelf of my bookshelf. She knew how special it was to me, and I wanted her to see it the most.

I stuck a sticky note on the outside of the empty notebook. It said: "See where fire with fire has gotten us. The other gift was much better.

See You When I See You." It didn't need a salutation. She'd know exactly who it came from.

On my way to work I stopped at her apartment. Like my apartment there was controlled access, so I had to sneak in through the parking garage below the building. I couldn't tell if there was anyone else in the building. I was still in a trance. To tell you the truth, I don't remember the trip to her doorstep at all. But I remember putting that box at her doorstep. I didn't set it flat. I leaned it against the door lengthwise so it would fall if someone opened the door. I had to make sure someone noticed it.

When I walked away from her door, all that was left to do was let her know her gift was there. I sent her a text message, I'd thought about what to say for a long time. I wrote the message in my mind again and again until the wording was perfect. "You lied to me for the last time. I left your birthday present on your front door. Whether or not you get it is no longer my problem." Maybe it was monstrous of me, but it still didn't seem like enough. I pulled my phone out and sent a second message: "Fuck you."

Chapter 5

It was a long time since Holt last rolled a joint, and twisting up a fatty was a far cry from riding a bike. He lacked the tools of his college days. Breaking up weed by hand was not nearly as effective as scissors or a grinder. As he broke it up he lost as much weed on his fingertips and the floor as ended up in his rolling pile. Normally, Holt was meticulous at everything he did, but alcohol fueled haste. He saw the sun getting lower in the sky, and he didn't want to miss the sun's water color fade over the ocean.

It took him several tries to get the roll down. The first time he tore the paper, and the time after that his drunken hands fumbled. Everything wound up on the floor and he had to use the hotel stationary to clean up the mess he made and start over. The third try was more successful, but he had the paper backward – an amateur mistake. By the fourth try he rolled something, but it would have been a bit of a stretch to call it a joint.

Outside there was a stiff breeze off the ocean bordering on wind. He dropped his artless work in the breast pocket of his shirt and crossed the street to the boardwalk. Holt liked walking in the soft New Jersey sand without shoes, but it was far too cold that night to walk barefoot. He paused at the edge of the boardwalk and looked down at his shoes. They cost him a fortune, and he knew the sand would destroy the hand-crafted, Italian leather. Since Holt didn't pack any clothes, he had nothing else to wear.

"Fuck it…they're just shoes. This is tradition."

Holt's feet sank into the soft sand as he stepped without fear of consequence. The loss of shoes was far less painful than the idea of lost opportunity, and there was no way to adequately enjoy the rhythmic sound of waves against the sand from the boardwalk. He cut across the beach toward the place where the ocean met the sand. Not only was the sand near the water easier to walk across, there the ocean was more enjoyable and his escape more complete. The crushing sound of the waves drowned out the world and Holt entertained himself by walking right against the edge of the water. He liked to play a game with the waves: running back and forth with the waterline as one wave fell back and a new one came in. As the water receded he stepped into its former territory. He followed the water toward the sea and watched for the next wave to break. The idea was to escape the returning water before his feet got wet. Before, when he and Sera lived near this very same beach, the stakes of the game were much lower. In those days his shoes were cheap and easy to dry. Tonight he had to take this game seriously or he may lose shoes that cost more than he made in a month when he was a bartender. He grew up in Kansas – far from the ocean – but there was something about the crashing sound and the competitive nature of the sea that drew him in. As he walked along the water, chasing and being chased by wave after wave, he pondered how he could invent a game the sea could be so good at. No matter how many times he played, the sea always managed to win at least once. That night, when he finally lost, the sandy water engulfed his feet inside the Italian leather and he laughed at the love he felt for the sea. It was an attraction he lost somewhere in a forest of skyscrapers towering over a meadow of yellow New York taxis; and, like love felt for any good woman, it took mere seconds for the sea to draw him in once again. It was a gravitational pull only matched by the smell of his wife's hair – more appropriately his soon-to-be ex-wife's hair.

Thoughts of his wife maneuvered his mind from competition to sadness. He looked for the horizon to his left, but the fading light made it impossible to tell where the sea ended and the sky began. His gaze moved up away from the hidden horizon across the night black sky over the point where black gave way to purple and purple to yellow and orange and red. He tried to distract himself from thoughts of Sera by exploring why all the colors of the rainbow were present in the light of the dying day except for the colors blue and green. Physics was in no way foreign to Holt, but it was a question that escaped his ability to answer. Blue was easy to explain: it was the color of day, and day must give way to night. But green was a more difficult enigma. Perhaps the lack of green in the early night sky had something to do with the color of chlorophyll – green inside the leaves of grass, trees, and other photo synthesizers. Or perhaps green light was unnatural. It could have been any one of a thousand reasons, but the fact of the matter remained the same. In the sequence of rainbow colors between red and violet there was no green to be seen in a storm-less sky. It may have been a

Chasing Angels

meaningless debate to have with himself, but it was better than clinging to thoughts of Sera.

Holt stopped walking to think about the sky. Maybe it was the alcohol and distracting thoughts of colors that stopped him in his sandy footprints. Maybe it was the fact that thoughts of Sera were the only thing that kept him moving forward since he was twenty-two. Luckily, his thoughts were interrupted by another wave crashing against his ankles. He took one last look over his head from east to west. Although he was only stationary for a moment or two, the black of night had moved a noticeable distance. It was almost the perfect time to start his ritual. He had to hurry up and get to his destination before night conquered the Jersey Shore.

He kept his eyes forward and stepped lightly against the sand. His eyes adjusted to the darkness as the light faded. Although the ocean and the sky blended together, the white sand stood out against the black water, lighting his way in the low light of a waning crescent moon. By the time the houses along the beach gave way to the open field of the National Guard shooting range, night was complete.

He stepped away from the shore and made his way to the end of a large concrete sea wall that divided the grassy range from the sand. Time crumbled the edge of the concrete where Holt took his seat. He pulled the joint from his pocket and dug out his lighter. He hit the flint and lit the twisted end. As he did so, little pieces of weed shot into his mouth.

"Fuckin' salad shooter. You're outta practice."

After taking a couple more hits, the light feeling of THC floated to his brain. He coughed after almost every hit, pushing his high higher. He jumped when his phone started vibrating in his pocket – half from paranoia and half from surprise. The number on the screen was immediately recognizable. It was Sera.

"Hey," he answered. "It's been a while."

"You're in New Jersey."

"I needed to talk to Mike."

"About what?"

"It doesn't matter. I'm leaving tomorrow."

Holt shifted in the sand when silence was the only sound in his phone. He had trouble reading Sera when they were on the phone. She

101

had the uncanny ability to maintain an even tone with every word, and she was smart enough to keep her statements short and to the point. Holt could read anyone's mind in any situation, but Sera figured out how to block his telepathy years ago. She was well aware that silence was Holt's biggest fear because it left him with only the ringing of Tinnitus in his ears. Sera could have been thinking anything on the other end, and Holt didn't like to talk to someone if he didn't know what was on their mind. It never bothered him before with Sera – in fact, he had always found the mystery of her thoughts endearing. Hers was the only mind he had to explore the old fashioned way. She was his kryptonite.

"Are you still there?" she asked.

"Yeah. I'm just trying to figure out what to say. We haven't talked in a while. I'm sorry."

"Don't apologize. It's weird for me, too. Where are you staying?"

"That same hotel we always stayed at down the street from Happy Hour."

"Gotta be within walking distance of your bar stool?" Sera laughed but Holt refused to laugh back. "What time are you leaving tomorrow?"

"I haven't gotten that far yet. I'm hanging out with Mike in the morning, but I don't know after that."

"Can I see you before you go?"

"I guess that would probably be a good idea. I brought the papers with me. We should probably just get it over with, you know. And I brought something I need you to sign. I'm closing the sale on the apartment next Friday. I can't complete the sale without your signature."

"You're selling the apartment?"

"I'm not living there without you."

"I guess that's fair. I'll give you mine…if you give me yours."

"Fair enough. Call me when you wake up." Holt ended the call as quickly as it interrupted his smoking session. He took another hit and watched the cherry creep closer to his lips.

He looked away toward the starry sky ahead of him. It was a view he forgot to miss in New York. Half a decade earlier, when he lived a couple miles away from the sea wall, he smoked there on a semi-nightly basis. Every day he saw this same sky full of stars and, on a nearly moonless night like that one, the number of stars increased exponentially with the receding phase of the moon. Every night in New York was starless. "What the hell was I thinkin' to leave this behi-?"

His light conversation was interrupted by movement to his left. A body passed underneath the street light a hundred yards up the beach. He instantly recognized the soda bottle figure behind crossed arms. Sera always walked like that, looking at the ground in front of her feet. Her eyes were poor so it was a waste for her to stare too far down her path. She only saw the world within a dozen steps. On the other hand, Holt's eyes were flawless at any distance within his line of sight. He panicked.

The light from the street lamp only covered a distance of ten yards in any direction. At most, it took Sera five seconds to cover that ground. By the time she did, Holt uprooted himself and hid among the sandy dunes behind the sea wall. He took one last puff off the joint and butted it out against the sole of his shoe. When he did, he heard Sera's steps on the wind. He saw her silhouette against the white sand as it passed between the nearest dune and the edge of the sea wall.

He heard her take a seat just behind him on the beach side of the sea wall where he sat moments before. He held still afraid any movement may clue Sera in on his presence. He would do anything for his wife, but he was nowhere near ready to see her. He had to put off seeing all the hate she had for him as long as he could.

"I must be crazy," she said. "I'm not ready to see you Holt. I just know the second I see you I'm gonna fall head over heels for you all over again and I can't do that. Not after you lied for so long. Why did you lie? One month – one month you were in Colorado without me, and all you had to do was put that envelope in the mail. But what did you do? Tell me you mailed it and hid it in the console of your truck for more than a decade.

"For the longest time I thought you stopped loving your truck and, because of that, you stopped loving everything else. I was wrong though. There were times I was scared you'd pick that old truck over me if faced with the choice. I knew the intense connection you had with that pickup because I shared that same connection with you. You killed your connection with that truck when you put it in storage to start driving a fucking Mercedes. You bought a new car every year and you used that truck to hide a lie. When you lied to me – to Mike and Cait – you stopped trusting me. When you stopped trusting me you started loving me less and less and the less you loved me the more you hated yourself. You turned into that asshole you wrote about in that first story you showed me back in college."

Sera's sobs drowned out the sounds of the wind and the waves. Holt pictured her shoulders heave with every heavy breath. He pictured the tears squeezed between her hands and her cheeks. He pictured the poorly painted finger nails as she ran them through her hair. With every frame of Sera's sadness in the motion picture of Holt's mind he pushed his head back hard against the sea wall. The love of his life – his soul mate – the one – the woman he loved so much the words themselves would sound unspeakably lame – was within arm's reach. The only thing that separated the two of them was a foot of concrete.

Holt clinched his fist as he kept hitting his head against the wall behind him. It would have been easier to walk around the wall to reach his wife, but that would distance him from her and her from him. More distance meant less gravity and her gravity felt so goddamn good. Instead, he tried to break through the wall with the back of his head. No matter how hard he tried the concrete held strong.

"It's not letting go that scares me. It's the hope that everything may work out that kills me. Jesus Christ, it smells like you're sitting next to me like when we used to come here. I hate how much I love you, Boy."

'Boy,' she had not called Holt by that name in years, but he knew she would have said something else if they were face to face. She would have called him Holt or Mr. Mallory or babe or any of a thousand mediocre names. Boy, on the other hand, had this terrible humanizing effect on Holt. Holt spent his whole life afraid he was something other than human, but that word was enough to make him just as vulnerable as every person on Earth. In the time it took the 'o' to cross from 'b' to 'y' and around the sea wall to Holt's ear his first tear of the night hit his cheek. He cried in silence with his wife, but she never knew. She never knew while she cried out loud a foot behind him. She never knew as she wiped her own tears away. She never knew as Holt watched her silhouette re-cross the space between the crumbled end of the sea wall and the dune behind which her shadow disappeared.

Holt held his breath to maintain his silence long after his wife walked away for fear that she may hear him on the wind. The sound of the waves against the shore returned along with the ringing in his ears.

The two sounds competed, each one fighting for dominance. Finally the ringing in his ears was so loud he no longer heard the sound of the ocean. But the ringing was not ringing anymore. Instead, the sound he thought was ringing turned out to be screams – his screams. He finally let loose to cry out loud. He punched the sand and whaled alone in the dark. He remembered the last time he cried himself to exhaustion, the night he told Sera about his dead parents at that same sea wall.

When Holt had no energy left to cry he crawled on fists and knees around the crumbled end of the sea wall. On the other side he saw the heart shape in the sand where Sera was just sitting. He took a seat next to her ass print to finish his smoke. But, when he opened the hand that held the joint – the joint he worked so hard to roll – the whole reason behind his ill fated trip to the sea wall – it was crushed, unsmokable in his palm.

Coming Soon

<u>Chasing Angels and Failing Aristotle</u>
<u>Volume 2: Renaissance Mind</u>

The soundtrack includes, but is not limited to:

"Easy"
"Cocaine"
"Colder Weather"
"Bad Company"
"Waiting in Vain"